COWBOYS, DOCTORS...
DADDIES!

*The Montgomery brothers—
from bachelors to dads!*

Trevor and Cole Montgomery
are the best-looking bachelors in
Cattleman Bluff—not to mention the doctors
everyone wants to see!

More than one woman has tried to persuade
these men to say 'I do', but no one's
succeeded... Until two women move to
Cattleman Bluff and turn the lives of
these hot docs upside down!

Because it's not just the women
Trevor and Cole are going to fall in love
with—it's their adorable children too...

Don't miss this delightful new duet
from Lynne Marshall:

Hot-Shot Doc, Secret Dad

and

Father for Her Newborn Baby

Available now!

Dear Reader,

Welcome to Cattleman Bluff, Wyoming!

When I first mentioned to my editor that I'd like to write about cowboy doctors, to be honest I expected a giggle. Instead I found support and enthusiasm for Trevor and Cole, the Montgomery brothers of Wyoming.

In Book One, *Hot-Shot Doc, Secret Dad*, Trevor literally gets the surprise of his life. Little does he know that the emphasis will be on 'family' when he hires Julie Sterling, a nurse practitioner returning to her hometown after being away for thirteen years. Funny how life has a way of sometimes putting us exactly where we belong…

A freak accident introduced Cole to medicine. He's the hero in Book Two, *Father for Her Newborn Baby*. When Cole has to step down from his highly respected position as a cardiology specialist and return to do country medicine for a while he's paired with Lizzie Silva, a 'rough around the edges' doctor from the streets of Boston. She comes with extra baggage…in the way of a tiny baby! Can things get any more complicated?

I'm proud to mention that this story is my twentieth book for Harlequin Mills & Boon®. I was thrilled to write two stories set in the gorgeous state of Wyoming, a place I love and can't wait to visit again. Plus, I got to write about not one but two weddings! I hope you enjoy the **Cowboys, Doctors…Daddies** duet as much as I enjoyed writing Trevor, Julie, Cole and Lizzie's stories.

Happy trails!

Lynne

www.lynnemarshall.com

'Friend' Lynne Marshall on Facebook to keep up with her daily shenanigans.

FATHER FOR HER NEWBORN BABY

BY
LYNNE MARSHALL

First published in Great Britain 2015
by Mills & Boon, an imprint of Harlequin (UK) Limited,
Eton House, 18-24 Paradise Road, Richmond, Surrey, TW9 1SR

© 2015 Janet Maarschalk

ISBN: 978-0-263-25903-2

Harlequin (UK) Limited's policy is to use papers that are natural, renewable and recyclable products and made from wood grown in sustainable forests. The logging and manufacturing processes conform to the legal environmental regulations of the country of origin.

Printed and bound in Great Britain
by CPI Antony Rowe, Chippenham, Wiltshire

Lynne Marshall used to worry that she had a serious problem with daydreaming—then she discovered she was supposed to write those stories! A late bloomer, Lynne came to fiction writing after her children were nearly grown. Now she battles the empty nest by writing stories which always include a romance, sometimes medicine, a dose of mirth, or both, but always stories from her heart. She is a Southern California native, a woman of faith, a dog-lover and a curious traveller.

Books by Lynne Marshall

Mills & Boon® Medical Romance™

Temporary Doctor, Surprise Father
The Boss and Nurse Albright
The Heart Doctor and the Baby
The Christmas Baby Bump
Dr Tall, Dark...and Dangerous?
NYC Angels: Making the Surgeon Smile
200 Harley Street: American Surgeon in London

**Visit the author profile page at
millsandboon.co.uk for more titles**

To John-Philip and Kaitlyn for helping me see magic
where a gnarly oak tree stood on that ranch.
Your wedding inspired me to write
a gorgeous scene for my characters.

And to granddaughter Thea
for being the inspiration for Flora.

Praise for
Lynne Marshall

'Heartfelt emotion that will bring you to the point of tears, for those who love a second-chance romance written with exquisite detail.'
—*Contemporary Romance Reviews* on
NYC Angels: Making the Surgeon Smile

'Lynne Marshall contributes a rewarding story to the *NYC Angels* series, and her gifted talent repeatedly shines. *Making the Surgeon Smile* is an outstanding romance with genuine emotions and passionate desires.'
—*CataRomance*

PROLOGUE

LIZZIE SILVA PUMPED the air. "Yes!"

I've got a job. Thank you, world! She glanced at Flora, nestled in her arm having just finished nursing, and then went completely still, afraid the sudden movement might set the baby off again. Maybe it had been the turmoil of her pregnancy, and stress and medical school had certainly taken a toll, but Flora had been born crying and had rarely stopped since. Or maybe it was because Flora sensed Lizzie didn't have a clue about being a mother. Her heart squeezed as it always did when she thought about that. But wouldn't things be better now?

She held her breath and lifted Flora to her shoulder and patted her back. "We're going to have our first adventure together," she cooed as Flora burped. "Good girl." As if the delivery and first three months of her daughter's life hadn't been adventure enough already.

She'd just ended a phone call with her favorite professor from medical school, the man who'd become a surrogate father, probably out of pity, or guilt, but nevertheless. Even now, since she'd broken up with his son, he was looking out for her and his granddaughter.

"We're moving to Wyoming. Can you imagine?" She smiled and rubbed her cheek against her baby's fuzzy head. So far, so good; Flora was sleeping. At last!

Never in her life had she felt such love. This precious little child would know how to trust because Lizzie promised with all of her heart never to let her down. Ever since Flora had been born, she'd dreamed of getting her out of the city, of giving her a better start than she'd had. Now this job opportunity had come out of nowhere, as if answering her prayer, and deep down she believed better things would follow if she said yes.

She'd walked off her last temporary job at the Boston clinic dealing with drug addicts. Especially when she'd had to counsel the meth head who was pregnant. It'd hit too close to home because of her own mother. Add in her new-parent stress and little sleep and she'd quit that very afternoon.

Flora suffered with colic and kept her up most nights, and Lizzie was always tired, but she'd never leave her daughter. She knew how it felt to be left behind as a baby by her mother, and ten years later by her grandmother, even though the dear woman couldn't control the stroke that had killed her. She knew the constant disappointment as foster home after foster home had let her go. Until she was fifteen and met Janie. Thank God for Janie, yet even she'd let her down. *Why did people choose to keep cancer a secret?* She would have dropped everything to be by her side. But then maybe that was what Janie had been afraid of. The woman had been intent on helping Lizzie get a hand up in life.

If it weren't for Janie Tuttle she'd never be a new graduate doctor, licensed and all. She never would have reached for the stars with a dream of going to college.

She cuddled Flora closer as the baby finally settled into deep sleep. She'd been at her wit's end all evening, as usual, not knowing what she was doing wrong, or why her baby cried so much. Not to mention worrying about how she'd support the two of them. She'd finally calmed Flora by nursing her again, then the cell phone had buzzed, and, as she'd often found herself doing at any little noise, she'd held her breath waiting for her daughter to start crying again. But this time she hadn't. Then the new temporary job offer had come. Beggars couldn't be choosers. Maybe this was a good omen?

No matter how much of a challenge this little one was, she loved how her child smelled and felt, and how she breathed unevenly. Basically, she loved everything about her, even when she was inconsolable with colic. Could the colic somehow be her fault? Mother's love cut to the center of her most sacred feelings. Poor kid got stuck with her. Tears welled in her eyes. "I'll never let you down, sweetheart. I promise. Never," she whispered, shaking. There was no way she'd ever be able to live up to that promise, since she basically didn't know what she was doing as a mother. Yet she hoped her unstoppable love would get through to her daughter.

Fear shuddered through her for her daughter's sake, as she worried that life might prove her wrong. This time she blamed it on postpartum hormones rather than her mounting insecurity as a parent. She had to face the fact she was a mess, a total wreck.

All the street smarts in the world couldn't make up for not having a clue how to be a mother, and the tough facade clearly didn't work with parenting.

She'd been anything but a skilled mother so far, feeling nothing short of a feeding machine, completely out of her depth. Due to Flora's colic, she functioned on minimal sleep; most days she felt like some kind of half monster, half human thing slogging through the hours. But so far they'd both survived. Somehow.

Becoming a mother had been a shock. Especially without backup. Dave Rivers had been another in a long list of disappointments, turning out to be nothing more than a biological father. And the most recent disappointment, not getting a residency at any of the hospitals where she'd applied, was further proof she was a screw-up. Then walking off the only job she could find...

She gingerly laid Flora in her cradle, held her breath again and watched the baby settle into deeper sleep. *Whew.* Lizzie sat on her own bed in the single-room apartment she'd rented all through medical school, trying her best not to make a single sound.

Panic had riddled her when she'd gotten the same rejection five different times. And she hadn't exactly been able to hit the pavement looking for work when she'd been about to pop with a baby on board, so she'd taken whatever she could get—the free clinic. She'd never felt more helpless in her adult life, but she'd gone into labor and become a mother, and now three months later was still trying to get her life back on track.

Lying back on her pillow, she willed the negative thoughts from her mind, choosing to take the opportunity to rest while Flora slept. She had a chance to start afresh, to give her baby an opportunity she'd never had. Dr. Rivers had promised the small medical clinic could accommodate her every need. She needed the job and believed it could be the start of a new life for her and her daughter. She needed that new start. *Please, please, make it so.*

Anxiety grabbed hold again. There was so much to do before Saturday when she'd board a plane for Wyoming and begin their new start.

Thank you, Dr. Rivers, for believing in me. And for helping these last few months.

She had a job.

Yes!

CHAPTER ONE

IT WAS COLE MONTGOMERY'S turn to step up for the family. He'd been absent far too long. While his brother, Trevor, was away he needed to oversee the ranch and help his father, the man he'd avoided most of his adult life. And because Cole was a doctor, he'd promised to keep the Cattleman Bluff Medical Clinic running while Trevor took a well-deserved honeymoon and vacation. At his sides, his fingers twitched. To be honest, he didn't know if he had what it took to take the reins at home, or the patience to deal with his father.

He stood off to the side of the wedding party, feeling more of a bystander than a part of the family. It was his younger brother, Trevor's turn to shine today, being the first of the brothers to marry. Plus, Trevor had a ready-made family with his beautiful new wife, Julie, originally a Cattleman Bluff girl, and the son Trevor never knew about until four months ago, James. At thirteen, the boy looked ecstatic, practically bouncing out of his skin, as he watched his parents finally take their vows.

What must it be like to get married and already have a family to look out for? If anyone could handle it, Trevor could, but the thought of raising kids sent a shudder from the tip of Cole's spine all the way down to his toes. Especially after his recent and total failure with Victoria and her five-year-old son, Eddie. Yeah, he'd pretty much proved his inability to be a boyfriend and potential father with that year-and-a-half dating nightmare.

Trevor and Julie's ceremony was intimate with only a handful of family and friends. They'd opted to have it in the silo portion of the ranch, the circular part smack in the middle of the house Dad had built around it. The silo had been their mother's art studio many years ago. Skylights made for perfect, almost magical lighting showering over his brother and the new bride, and seemed like a posthumous blessing from their mother who'd died several years ago. Cole knew she would have loved every moment of this simple yet ideal ceremony. There'd been a reason she'd chosen this section of the house to paint her pictures.

He took a moment to remember his mother, the peacemaker. She'd had to work extra hard when Cole was a teenager, since he and his father seemed to butt heads on every little detail in life. His dad wanted to train him to take over the ranch when the time came, and all Cole had wanted to do was show off at junior rodeos. After the accident, when his father pushed him to spend weeknights learning the ins and outs of cattle ranching, Cole had signed up for the high-school academic decathlon, which assured he wouldn't have an extra minute to learn anything from his father. And that earned him the nickname of Wonder Boy, said with contempt not pride by his father.

When Cole eventually announced he wanted to be a doctor, not a cowboy, well, Tiberius hadn't been able to hide the disappointment. What father in his right mind got upset when his son wanted to go into medicine?

A "cantankerous old cowboy first, father second" kind.

Cole wished his mother were here so he could hug her and tell her how much he'd always loved her. But rather than slide into a sentimental slump, he shifted his gaze from the overhead skylights back to the bride.

Julie Sterling, soon-to-be Montgomery, looked stunning in an off-white cocktail-length dress, her unruly brown hair piled high on her head, dotted with baby's breath and tiny yellow daisies, making her big eyes look nothing short of huge. He couldn't help but notice she had great legs, too—Trevor's favorite part of female anatomy. And by the way she looked at his brother, that wide stare was meant only for him. A good thing.

Cole wondered what that might be like—had a woman ever only had eyes for him? It seemed there was always a link to his accomplishments, or a secret wish for what he could offer, and when those things got stripped away, the love light fizzled out. That was how it had worked with Victoria when he'd never gotten around to proposing. He glanced at his lucky-dog brother.

Trev looked nothing short of dignified in his Western tux and new boots, and Cole hadn't exactly held up his end of the bargain if he was supposed to dress in kind. Instead, he'd opted for one of his tailor-made city suits, the type he wore for fund-raisers or exclusive speeches, of which, in his new role as cardiac educator, there were many.

He continued to study his brother, a refined version of himself. Where Cole had inherited his father's rugged, rangy looks, Trevor had the luck of their mother's delicate features blended in with the coarse Montgomery genes. Mom's DNA might have cut a couple inches off Trevor's height, making Cole a truly "big" brother, but the good looks and confidence his little brother possessed had sure worked wonders in life, and especially with the ladies. Always had. Being six years older than Trevor, Cole had never felt particularly close to the kid, even though his brother had always looked adoringly up to him. Was it any wonder they'd both become doctors? Yeah, Dad sure loved that, too. He ran his hand over his short hair, noting Trevor had let his grow out a bit more, maybe at

Julie's request? Who knew the influence a woman could have over a man.

He sure didn't. None of his relationships had ever come close to love or commitment. He blamed it on his job. His single-minded quest to improve cardiology, to take mitral-valve replacements to a new level. His success. His laziness? Or maybe it went all the way back to being fifteen, when Hailey Brimley, the first girl he'd ever loved—and the girl he'd literally broken his neck for—had taken one look at him all banged up with rods sticking out of his skull and walked out of the hospital never to come back. He'd risked everything for young love and she hadn't been able to get past how he'd looked in that damned halo brace. Yeah, there was that link to accomplishment, or lack of, even back then. Whatever the reason, at forty, he was a single guy with zero prospects for true love, and watching his brother get married forced him to think about his own circumstances. Well, guess what, that was how he liked it. Single. Unattached. *Sorry, Victoria, but that's the truth.* Busy with his career. He cleared his throat and straightened the knot of his silk necktie. At least that was his side of the story and he was sticking with it.

His father, Tiberius, stood to the right of Cole as the couple took their vows. With one hand on the carved wooden walking stick—since he'd chucked his clunky quad cane for the ceremony—his father was decked out in his finest Wyoming duds, including his prized Stetson, which he'd removed and held with his free hand for the duration of the ceremony. Cole noticed something he hadn't seen in years: a contented smile on his father's face. He'd personally stopped seeing that look when he'd shown off for a girl at the high school rodeo and had broken his neck. Twenty-five years ago. Or maybe it was when he'd flat out told his old man he never wanted to be a stinkin' cattle rancher. But today was a day of celebration, and

Cole didn't want to focus on the past. So he shifted his gaze once again, and looked to the future.

James, Julie's son, grinned as if he knew the world's biggest secret and was about to share it. Personally, the thought of raising a teenager, or any kid, in today's world made Cole shiver inside, but since the boy's happiness was palpable and proved to be contagious he joined in and smiled. Why not? He was at a wedding. His brother's wedding.

The couple pledged their unending love and kissed, and soon the crowd of twenty broke out in a cheer. Cole applauded and gave his nearly forgotten rodeo whistle, adding to the noise reverberating off the circular silo walls.

Though it was a special day for Trevor and Julie, Cole felt somehow uninvolved, holding back to himself. Truth was he didn't have a clue what to expect filling in at the Cattleman Bluff Medical Clinic, which, thanks to his brother's extended honeymoon and family-bonding trip, would take up almost his entire summer. Cole had taken a leave of absence to accommodate their trip. As he'd known in his gut, it was time to step up for the family.

The couple had waited until the school semester ended for James before they got married, thus the mid-June wedding. They planned a weeklong honeymoon in Montreal while James went back to LA with his great-aunt Janet. The week after that they'd go out to LA to pick up James and to take in some tourist sights, then they'd all come home and head off on a monthlong road trip around Wyoming, camping, hiking, fishing, horseback riding, anything they felt like doing, but most of all bonding. That was the word Trevor had used over and over while telling Cole his plans. He didn't know the whole story since he and his brother had hardly had a minute together before the wedding, but Trevor and his son sure had a lot of lost time to make up for.

The wedding party had moved on to the second champagne toast, and everyone suddenly looked towards Cole. He hadn't given a single notion to what he should say, so he thought quickly. "I want to wish the bride and groom as much happiness as our own dad and mother had in their marriage. Love doesn't run any deeper than that. Cheers!"

Cole caught a glimpse of his father's tearing eyes as the man raised his glass and toasted new love along with everyone else, while most likely remembering the loss of his own. His dad had fallen apart when Mom died from cancer. His life had literally stopped, and, though he'd tried to pick up the pieces over the past several years, his health had never been the same. That kind of love scared the hell out of Cole. Was that what Trevor was setting himself up for, too? Another good reason for Cole to stick with his current life trajectory.

Bittersweet moments clogged his throat, and he didn't have a clue why that tended to happen much more often when back home. He didn't like it—those deep feelings, the kind that ripped at a person's heart. Maybe that was why he preferred his hundred-mile buffer zone, living out in Laramie half the time and in Baltimore the other, except whenever he was on the road, which seemed to be close to 80 percent of the time lately.

He took another drink of champagne. Staying put for two months in the house he'd grown up in, seeing the continuing disappointment and blame in his father's milky, aging eyes, and sensing the lingering love from his mother would prove to be a challenge. How long before he and his father finally had it out?

The old man's health was failing; he grew weaker by the year yet still insisted on running the ranch. Cole couldn't very well blast him with accusations and force an apology, could he? Damn, he needed more champagne.

When everyone else was joining in with the celebration, laughing, cheering, making a racket, Cole slipped a little farther back from the crowd. Julie prepared to toss the bouquet, and once she turned her back and threw the flowers over her head, the dozen or so ladies in the group started to squeal. The young blonde from the medical clinic, Rita the receptionist, caught it and screamed with delight. Her glittering eyes flitted toward his, and he quickly looked away, deciding now was the perfect time to refill his glass with bubbly.

Briefly, while on his quest for the server, he engaged Jack, the ranch foreman, in conversation. He felt him out as to how the family business was holding up, assuring Jack he'd be as helpful as possible in Trevor's absence. In fact, Cole looked forward to getting on a horse again. The rodeo had been his passion in life throughout his childhood and early teens. He'd made a name for himself on the junior circuit, riding bucking broncos, until...

"Incoming!" he heard Jack say.

Cole looked up in time to reach up and pluck a shiny white lace garter out of the air, rather than let it hit him in the face. *What the—?* He glanced up at his brother's mischievous dark stare, a smile stretched from ear to ear. Was that a challenge?

"You're next, Cole," Trevor said, laughing, knowing full well the absurdity of the remark.

Playing along, only to be polite, Cole mock kissed the garter, then stuck it in his handkerchief pocket. "I'll keep you posted, Trev, but don't hold your breath." He made a shrewd effort to avoid Rita's coy gaze at all costs.

He got his refill of champagne and finished it with three large gulps, enjoying the floating-in-water feeling in his head.

When he was a kid, he used to think the sky in Wyoming was the limit, and anything was possible on any given day. Wasn't that why they'd called him Wonder Boy?

These days, not so much. Still smiling, since everyone seemed to continue to stare at him, he hoisted yet another glass in another toast. "Cheers!" he said as expected, waggling his brows, as any lucky guy who'd just caught the garter on a glorious wedding day should. Then he took one more drink of champagne, letting that pleasant buffer of booze make everything fuzzy around the edges, and followed the crowd outside for the reception and lunch.

Tomorrow he'd saddle up and ride the range with Jack. He couldn't remember the last time he'd ridden the entire Circle M Ranch or seen the thousands of head of pure English-bred steer roaming the grasslands, and, being honest, he'd missed it. Of course, he'd need a refresher course on the challenges of raising grass-finished cattle for meat. His father's specialty. Genetics was the key, his old man had always said, and, being a scientist, Cole could easily wrap his brain around that. But all the finer details of animal husbandry he'd leave to Jack.

As for right now, he couldn't very well zone out on the rest of his brother's wedding party, so he stood, straightened his tie and headed toward Trevor's table to tell him not to worry about a thing while he was on his honeymoon. His mother would want it that way.

"Just the man I need to talk to," Trevor said, eyes brightening as Cole approached his table.

"I thought you'd already told me everything I need to know." Cole had a sudden sinking feeling.

"I lined up some extra help for you at the clinic while I'm gone."

Cole wasn't about to complain about that. "Thanks. Someone from Cattleman Bluff?"

"Boston."

"What?"

"It's a complicated story, but, medically speaking,

the doctor is qualified. Lawrence Rivers highly recommended her."

Larry Rivers was a respected professor who'd mentored Trevor during medical school, and he'd become a trusted colleague for Cole when he'd made the decision to learn transcatheter heart-valve replacement. "But?" Cole's instincts waved yellow flags, waiting for Trevor to come clean with the rest of the story.

"The problem is, she only applied for internal medicine residencies at the top five most competitive hospitals in the country, so she didn't get a single spot."

"She's fresh out of medical school? And that's supposed to be a help, how?"

"You know Larry wouldn't recommend her if he didn't believe in her."

"Believing in and actually being competent are two different things." Ah, hell, Cole didn't want to get in an argument with his brother at his wedding. Mom wouldn't like that. He'd back off for now.

"She might be a little rough around the edges."

Are you kidding me? "You're joking, right? Is this some sort of weird wedding joke?"

"Larry said she's a tough Boston girl, from the wrong side of the Charles River. She can handle anything."

"So Larry's playing both of us, right?"

Trevor bit his lower lip and grimaced. "She needed a job. I said she could have it. You'll need help at that clinic, trust me."

"And I want all the help I can get, but—"

"Come on, Trevor," Julie said, a huge smile on her face, a warning gaze in her eyes. "It's time to change clothes for the send-off. The limo is going to be here in twenty minutes."

Trevor lifted his brows, cast a quick glance at Cole, then put his arm around his new wife.

"What's this doctor's name?"

"Elisabete Silva."

Great, he'd be working with a wet-behind-the-ears doctor who probably thought she knew it all. Didn't he think the same thing when he'd first graduated from medical school?

Trevor was the most conscientious man Cole knew, and wouldn't set him up for failure. Instead of acting like his father, blowing a gasket before getting the whole story, he'd take his mother's approach. He'd reserve his opinion until he'd met the new doctor at the clinic himself, but he suddenly had a kink in his gut that had nothing to do with the baked chicken served at the wedding-reception dinner.

Trevor started to walk off with Julie, but turned back. "Oh, one more thing. The doctor will be living here at the ranch. Dad said it's okay."

What in the hell was going on?

Trev looked as if he wanted to say something else, but Julie snagged him firmly by the elbow and led him off. Cole stood and watched as they headed off to change clothes while those waving yellow flags in his head started turning red.

Ten minutes after tossing rice and grinning along with everyone else, then watching the new couple drive off in the fully decorated "Just Married" limo, Cole saw a town car heading up the long road. The Circle M Ranch wasn't exactly on the main highway—anyone coming out this way generally had a reason.

He looked on with interest from the yard as the car came to a stop in front of the house and Jack, his father's ranch foreman, along with the family cook, Gretchen, rushed toward it.

"Cole, come and dance with me." Rita, the attractive blonde medical-clinic receptionist, linked her arm through his, her still-lingering potent perfume overpowering his nostrils. "It's tradition for the bouquet and garter catchers to have a dance together."

First he'd ever heard of that tradition. Cole didn't want to come off as impolite at his brother's wedding reception—his mother would be disappointed—especially since he'd be working with Rita all summer, so he let her lead him to the dance floor, losing sight of the limousine and the house as he did.

CHAPTER TWO

THE LAST OF the wedding guests had finally left. It was getting dark, and Cole had handed the mantle to the lead of the cleanup crew. He'd done his brotherly duty for Trevor's wedding, and looked forward to getting out of his suit and unwinding with a good novel before calling it a night.

He wandered toward the porch and the front door. Gretchen, the family cook, met him with an anxious look.

"Hello, Cole," she said, trying to sound calm but not coming close.

"Hi. What's up?" He remembered the limousine from earlier. "We have company?"

"Uh, yes." She wouldn't look him in the eyes.

"Is something wrong?" He stopped and waited for Gretchen to look up.

"Uh. No. I was just a little surprised, that's all." Still not looking at him, she turned toward the screen door.

"Surprised? About what?"

Tiberius appeared on the other side of the screen. "That she has a baby, that's what."

"Who has a baby?" His feet stuck to the porch floorboards.

"The doctor Trevor hired," his father said with a lopsided grin.

"A baby?" What was going on? The new doctor was here already?

"You know, the little tykes in diapers, a baby." His dad seemed to take great joy in rubbing in the news, though he looked tired beyond his years just then. It'd been a long few days preparing for the wedding; Cole would cut him some slack. "They cry a lot and need undivided attention?"

Cole sped up the last few steps to the front door, pulling out his cell phone on the way, ready to speed-dial his brother. "Trevor didn't mention that." In all honesty, Trevor hadn't had the chance.

"Of course not, because you would have thrown a fit if he did," Dad said, not splitting hairs, holding the door open for Gretchen and him to go inside.

"That's not necessarily true. But it would have been nice to know."

Before he could press dial, a tall and slender, dark-haired woman with vivid green eyes and ivory skin appeared in the entryway. She'd come from the east wing where she must have left her baggage, and had some sort of swaddling sling across her torso with a good-sized bulge buried inside.

"Hello," she said, a natural rasp in her lower-than-usual female voice. "I'm Elisabete, but everybody calls me Lizzie."

Out of the blue, Cole wondered how her laugh would sound. He guessed smoky and…

She reached out a thin hand with long delicate fingers, and, instead of dialing Trevor to curse him out, Cole pocketed the phone, took her hand and shook. Warmth emanated from both her grip and her wide gaze, which was truly stunning, and stole some of his thunder.

"I'm Cole. Nice to meet you. I'm a bit surprised by your…er…bundle there." He nodded to the lump dangling snuggly from her middle.

She gave a fatigued smile and glanced down beneath fuller-than-usual dark brows at her baby. "My little Flora screamed the entire flight from Boston. I think she's worn herself out. At one point I thought the flight attendant wanted to shove me out the door." She lifted her gaze, tension dwelling in those lovely, though bewildered, eyes even as she tried to make light of her situation. "I'll carry my load at the clinic, Dr. Montgomery. I promise."

Had she read his mind? Only then did he think to let go of the comfort of her hand. Those deeply inquisitive eyes studied him, obviously hunting for a sign of his humanity.

"With an infant that will be a huge challenge. Are you sure you can handle the job?"

"I don't know how much Dr. Rivers told you—"

"Dr. Rivers spoke to my brother, who left for his honeymoon today. I don't have a clue if Trevor knew about the bambino part or not." So much for his humanity.

"I've made some tea—why doesn't everyone sit down and I'll bring it?" Gretchen said, having never been able to handle tension, even though, having worked for years for the Montgomery family, she should have gotten used to it by now.

"Yes, why don't we?" Tiberius said, an amused smirk on his face. He led the way to the living room.

Cole gestured for Lizzie to follow, noting her jeans-clad long legs, narrow hips and flip-flop-covered feet, thinking how impractical the footwear was for a ranch. But there was something else he noticed beyond her travel-weary appearance, and besides the single long, thick braid down her back: it was the confidence with which she walked. The way she held her head high even under his less-than-gracious welcome. This one was a fighter. Maybe she had to be.

"What kind of name is Silva?" Tiberius asked just before he sat in his favorite overstuffed chair.

"It's Portuguese."

Cole wasn't exactly sure what he'd signed on for taking over his brother's practice, but, with the arrival of Lizzie sporting a baby, that task had suddenly gotten a hell of a lot more challenging.

While Gretchen served tea in the living room, Cole asked Lizzie about medical school, but got distracted with the dozens of other questions flying through his head.

"And after spending a month in the emergency department, I knew for a fact I didn't have what it takes to work under that kind of pressure. That place made me wicked crazy," she said without seeming to take a breath. "Internal medicine seemed the right fit for me. It's kind of like taking a good mystery—the patient's symptoms—and step-by-step solving the case by diagnosing and treating them properly. Makes me feel like a medical sleuth, kind of like that TV show, *House*, you know? So I'm really looking forward to working in your clinic, Dr. Montgomery."

Just what he needed, his own *House*. Didn't she understand that guy would have lost his medical license a hundred different times because of his antics? Cole definitely had his work cut out for him training a new, dreamy-eyed doctor.

Plus, she spoke rapid-fire, with a thick Bostonian accent, and to be honest he often had trouble following her. *Depahtmint. Pressha. Lookin' farwid.* But it was kind of amusing at the same time. He suppressed a smile as she talked on and on, probably nervous and wanting to make a good first impression. Meanwhile, he grasped for ways to make this situation work. New doctor. New mother. New clinic. And he'd thought he was out of his depth taking over the clinic before!

For a new mother, she certainly seemed to have a lot of energy, or maybe she was just a hyper type. He hoped she wouldn't talk his ear off all the time because that would get old fast. *Gee, thanks for sticking me with your sight-unseen doctor, Trev, old buddy.*

She continued on with her story, and Cole hoped she'd get around to mentioning the baby, but she conveniently skipped over that part. Instead she talked about experiences in medicine and kept assuring him she'd carry her load at the clinic, then stopped midsentence when her eyes settled on Tiberius, who still had an amused smirk on his face.

"Is that how you always smile?" she asked bluntly.

Granted, it was an odd lopsided smile, but Cole figured it was typical of Dad to be a smart aleck over the mixed-up circumstances Cole had found himself in. Then he looked closer. She was right: something was off.

Lizzie popped up from the chair and walked straight to his father. "Smile again," she said. "Hmm. Give me your hands. Squeeze." She glanced over her shoulder at Cole, her full arched brows raised, then quickly back to Tiberius. "Are you feeling numbness or tingling on either side?" Tiberius looked confused. "Cole, he's noticeably weaker on the right. Is this always the case?"

Cole jumped up and strode toward his father and Lizzie. "No."

"Raise your arms for me, Mr. Montgomery." The right arm went only half as high as the other. "Can you say 'the sky is blue'?"

It came out slurred and jumbled. "Sy…boo."

"I'll call 911." Cole dug for the phone in his pocket and made the call.

"He seemed to walk in here just fine, but then I noticed his droopy smile." Lizzie went down on her knees to look Tiberius in the eyes. "Is your vision blurry?"

He made a tiny shake of his head.

"He needs thrombolytics ASAP. Time is brain," she said, slipping into doctor mode, stating the obvious door-to-IV necessity for early treatment. "We've got a three-hour window."

Cole filled in the emergency operator. "We need a stroke team ready to go," he said when he'd finished. She assured him an ambulance would be on the way with estimated time of arrival twenty minutes. The nearest hospital was in Laramie. He did the math and knew time was of the essence if they wanted the best results with his father's evolving stroke. Panic ripped through him at the thought of losing his dad. He went to him and squeezed his shoulder. "We'll get the help you need, Dad."

Tiberius glanced up, seeming a bit disoriented. Trevor's wedding had taken more of a toll than Cole had realized.

"We should give him an aspirin right now," Lizzie said.

"He's already on daily aspirin."

"Let's give him another. Research shows the benefits outweigh the risk of causing bleeding in the brain."

Cole also knew this was an ongoing debate among clinicians. Some researchers said early aspirin was beneficial, others said it could prove risky. The key was whether a clot or a burst vessel was the cause of his father's stroke, and only a CT scan could prove that. Yet, the overemphasis of TPA, tissue plasminogen activator, as the only treatment could also cause bleeding in the brain. He wasn't about to take up that debate now with Lizzie when his father was in the middle of a stroke.

"Out of…" Tiberius mumbled.

What? "You're out of something?" Cole repeated what he thought his father meant.

"Asp." He looked and sounded like someone who'd just had Novocain injections at the dentist.

His father had a history of TIAs, transient ischemic attacks, and that was caused by blockage. Why hadn't he gotten a new bottle of aspirin immediately? Cole wanted to wring his dad's neck, but quickly remembered there'd been a lot of activity going on over the past week with wedding plans and parties and Cole moving back home. Today's wedding had been an all-day affair. He'd cut his father some slack, but still wondered if this TIA could have been prevented, and whether or not it would turn into a full-blown cerebrovascular accident this time around. The thought sent a shard of fear deep into his chest.

"Let's do it, then," Cole said, jogging to the closest medicine cabinet in the hall bathroom. "There isn't any here," he called out. Frustration blended with panic.

"I've got some in the kitchen," Gretchen said, close on his heels. "You should have told me you were out, Monty," she called over her shoulder.

When they returned, Lizzie had remained with Tiberius, reassuring him and distracting him by showing her newborn to him. She cooed over her baby and smiled up at the man. That lopsided smile returned, and his eyes looked calmer and more focused since gazing at the sleeping child.

"Take this, Dad." Cole gave him the aspirin. "Can you swallow okay?" He tested his dad with a tiny sip from the cup of forgotten tea on the table next to his chair. He seemed to swallow okay, so Cole gave it to him. If this was a true TIA, his symptoms would go away within ten to twenty minutes. If it was a CVA, there was no telling how long or how much worse it could get. By Cole's count it had already been over ten minutes since Lizzie had astutely noticed his father's quirky grin, and as of now the symptoms remained unchanged. A foreboding shadow settled around Cole's vision; worry kicked up the fear he'd tried to suppress. He wasn't ready to lose his dad. Nowhere near.

"I'm calling the Laramie ER, giving them a preliminary report. I already told them to have the stroke team ready to go the second Dad arrives."

"Do you have a blood-pressure monitor in the house?" Lizzie asked as he dialed his cell phone.

It'd been so long since Cole had lived here, he didn't rightly know.

"There's one in Monty's bedroom," Gretchen said, setting off in that direction of the house.

Cole studied his father, then looked at the beautiful baby with a full head of dark hair, just like her mother. The child squirmed and stretched while still deeply asleep, and that simple marvel kept that odd smile on his father's face. Whatever helped or distracted him. The man must be scared as hell of having another stroke. He prayed their actions would be enough for now.

Gretchen produced the portable blood-pressure cuff while Cole gave his report to the ER. He watched as Lizzie carefully placed her baby, who was obviously still exhausted from the big airplane trip, across Tiberius's lap, then she went right to work setting up and checking the numbers. "Well, we can't blame his blood pressure for this CVA." At one hundred and thirty over eighty-five it wasn't greatly elevated.

Cole repeated the BP to the doctor on the phone. He knew that eighty percent of all strokes were ischemic, caused by a blockage of blood flow. The fact that his father had kept his blood pressure under control since his first TIA a couple of years ago, plus his BP wasn't exceptionally high right now, meant the odds of a hemorrhagic stroke were much less. But you never knew, he couldn't be too cautious and the man belonged in the hospital for treatment and best outcome. And just before he finished the call, there was the sweet sound of a distant ambulance siren.

"Our ride's here," he said to the doctor on the other end, then gave his dad a reassuring smile. "ETA an hour and ten." That left a one- to two-hour window to get his father on thrombolytic therapy for best chance of full recovery. He hoped it would be enough.

CHAPTER THREE

WELL AFTER MIDNIGHT, Lizzie struggled with her colicky baby. These fits always seemed to happen at night. The child had been so intent on crying she couldn't calm down enough to nurse. At the end of her tether, Lizzie walked the floor of the cathedral-ceilinged living room, with the spiral staircase winding up to a huge loft library at the back.

She had no business being a mother. Didn't this prove it? She didn't know what she was doing, and poor Flora sensed it. The baby bore the brunt of her overworked and undertrained parent. She wanted to cry right along with her child, but held it in, afraid if she let that gate open she'd never regain control.

She'd put on quite a show that afternoon, walking into a strange house with her baby, acting as if she were the most confident girl in the world. Oh, yeah, move out of state? Take a temporary job? Piece of cake. *How long before Cole Montgomery sees through me?*

Headlights flashed across the arched, church-sized window. Oh, great, just what she needed—now Cole would know what a failure she was as a mother, too. She thought about running off to her room set away from the rest of the house. Maybe he wouldn't hear Flora's wails there. But her curiosity about Tiberius overpowered her desire to run and hide—was saving face really that important?—so she stayed put. Her one hope being Cole wouldn't demand she shut Flora up because if he did, she might have to quit the job before she even started.

She took a deep breath and switched her little one to the other arm and bounced her. Maybe Flora had worn herself out, because she shifted from scream mode to fussy and generally unhappy—an improvement. But could Lizzie blame her for having colic? The poor kid was stuck with her, clueless and unnatural, as a mother.

This move to Wyoming was supposed to be the first step in a better life for both of them, yet Flora's distress seemed to prove otherwise. Why did she have to doubt herself at every turn since becoming a mother? She couldn't very well ask her own mother for help.

A key turned the lock in the front door, and from the darkened room Lizzie saw Cole enter. His head immediately turned to the sounds of the baby's cries.

"Hi," she said, walking toward him, glad she'd thrown a long sweater over her funky flannel pajama pants and overstretched tank top. It was too late to try to do anything with her hair, though.

He nodded, looking tired and grim when he turned on the light. He watched her a few moments as they both adjusted to the sudden brightness.

"How's your dad?" She shifted Flora to her shoulder and rubbed her back as she continued to fuss loudly and squirm in her arms.

"He's stable. The CT scan showed blockage without bleeding, so that's good. They put him on ATP well within the window for best results. Only time will tell."

She thought about the news. It was promising, and that was all they could hope for tonight. "So the CVA hasn't evolved?"

"You still can't understand him when he tries to talk,

but the right-sided weakness seems less. At least that's something." Cole threw his keys in a ceramic bowl on the long entry hall table, the sound startling Flora and the fussing turned to crying. "Oh, sorry." He grimaced.

"It's not you. We've been up for a couple hours. I keep hoping she'll wear herself out enough so I can nurse her." God, she wanted to cry, that familiar helpless feeling of not being able to comfort her daughter ripping at her heart.

His brows pulled downward. "You need your sleep just as much as she does." Surprising her, he took off his jacket, laid it over the back of a chair and reached for Flora. "Maybe a change in scenery will help. Give her to me." He took her squirming baby, now looking amazingly tiny in his big hands and arms. "Let's go in the kitchen, and have some herbal tea or something. It'll do us both good."

He led the way—her wriggling, loudly protesting baby leaving him unfazed—and, though feeling embarrassed about her appearance, she followed. Fortunately the kitchen light had a dimmer, so Cole left it at half the usual brightness. That worked for Lizzie. The less he saw of her bed hair and unwashed face, the better.

"I'll put the water on," she said, noticing that Flora still fussed but had quieted down a little. "Where do you keep the tea?" In a kitchen the size of her entire apartment back in Boston, she didn't have a clue where to begin to look.

"The pantry," he whispered, and pointed to the corner, Flora in the crook of his elbow as he unconsciously rocked the fidgety baby. "Second shelf. I like the Sweet Dreams brand, but there's some chamomile, too, somewhere, I think."

It tickled her to think of big ol' Cole Montgomery liking herbal tea and holding babies. Even though he gazed at Flora as if she were an alien from Planet X. After she got the tea she was grateful the cabinets had glass doors, so at least she knew where to find the cups.

Behind her, he chuckled softly. "I think she's hungry— she keeps trying to suckle my neck."

"Oh!" Maybe she should stop everything and nurse that child since that seemed to be her message.

"You have a bottle or something?"

"I'm nursing. Why don't you give her to me?"

He gently handed Flora back to Lizzie, and their gazes caught and held briefly. He seemed to have questions in his, and she didn't want to begin guessing what he wondered. Most likely something along the lines of—*what in the hell are you doing here?*

Good question. Would he believe her answer—*making a better life for my daughter?*

Flora had settled down and showed all the signs of finally being ready to nurse. "If you don't mind watching the kettle, I'll take her back to the living room. I'm already in love with your dad's favorite chair."

He blinked his reassurance. "I'll bring the tea when it's ready."

Five minutes later, with Flora finally nursing contentedly, Lizzie had thrown her sweater over her chest for privacy, and Cole brought two teacups to the living room, lit only by the light of the moon.

"Mind if I join you?" he whispered.

She smiled up at him as he put her cup on the table nearest her free hand. She'd honestly expected him to use a mug, but he sat across from her and sipped his tea as if it was second nature. She couldn't think of a single thing to say to him because her main thought was, *Thank goodness Flora quit crying and is nursing.* Now maybe she could breathe. At least she knew how to do *something* good for her baby. Yet, hadn't Cole calmed the child down? Maybe he had a kid of his own?

"How do you know how to quiet babies so well?"

"I didn't know I did." His surprised-bordering-on-shocked expression said it all. Pure luck, the kind Flora wished she had more of. "I just saw you struggling and you looked like you needed some help." And wasn't that an understatement?

Her first sip of hot tea soothed her strained throat. It never ceased to amaze her how her entire body tensed when Flora was unhappy. She was surprised her milk let down so easily under the circumstances. "I thought maybe you had your own kids or something."

He let go a big puff of air, a sound meant to show the absurdity of the comment. "*No-o-o.* No kids. No wife. Just me and cardiology. See, I understand the physiology of the heart perfectly—the emotional side of things, don't have a clue."

She lightly laughed. "I hear you on that one." Cole had revealed a lot in that last sentence. Maybe they had something in common.

"So is that why you're not married either?"

Sitting in the dark helped shadow her first reaction—pain. A year ago she would have bet her life on her and Dave getting married, but, after his wicked change in character when she'd told him she was pregnant, she was glad she wasn't married to him. In fact, her life, or losing it, might have actually been part of the bet. The guy had gone ballistic with the news. He'd flipped out and grabbed her, shaking her violently, then shoved her against a wall, banging her head several times on the surface. *You think you can trap me with a kid? Think again.* She'd never seen him so crazed; the memory of his wild-eyed stare still sent shivers through her muscles.

She'd never felt more helpless in her life either and vowed that would never happen again. Fortunately, he'd stopped at roughing her up, hadn't hit her or anything, just manhandled her to frighten her for messing with his plans. He'd given her one last shake and left. So much for true love. And so much for never feeling helpless again. It seemed since Flora had been born, helpless had become her middle name.

She reminded herself she'd come to Wyoming to change things. She wasn't helpless. She had a job. "Her dad and I couldn't work things out. He took off. I stayed pregnant."

"How'd you manage to finish med school with a newborn?"

"Called in a lot of favors." It wasn't that she wanted to be abrupt, but, really, they didn't have all night for her to explain that one. Maybe the guy deserved a bit more than her glib answer, though. "When you're raised in foster care you learn to be resourceful. I'd helped a lot of students through the toughest modules, did one-on-one study sessions with a girl who probably would have failed the boards otherwise. You know, that kind of thing. They owed me."

"Wait a second, back up." He leaned forward. "You were raised in foster care?"

"After my grandmother died, yes." So she wasn't exactly being forthcoming. It wasn't that she wanted to be secretive; she was just saving him the sob story. Did Cole really need to hear all of it?

"And what happened to your mother?"

"She went back to being a meth head after I was born."

He shook his head and, since her eyes had adjusted to the dark, she could make out his sympathetic expression, brows pushed together, lips tight. Yeah, she'd had a hard life, he got it, no need to pound home the point. "And you rose above all of that and made it into medical school. That's amazing."

She pushed her head back onto the soft cushion of the high-backed chair, suddenly needing that extra comfort.

Put that way, yeah, maybe she was amazing. "The only thing I had control of in my childhood was my school grades. I guess you could say it paid off. If you don't count the fact that I wasn't chosen for a single residency program I applied for." She didn't want to sound sorry for herself, but the discouraged sigh had already left her lips.

"Didn't anyone counsel you on casting your net wide? From what I was told you only applied to the five most prestigious hospitals in the nation. No offense, but what were you thinking?"

"That I should reach for the stars." She needed to shut him down, be blunt, because she'd gone over her blunder a million times already and it always came back to the same conclusion—there was nothing she could do about that now. And that was why she'd come to Wyoming, to make up for it. To start over. To give her baby a good start in life.

Her little scientific experiment had worked. She'd formed her hypothesis, tested it, and analyzing her data—sitting in silence, the dim light from the hallway making his shadow large and looming, mouth firmly shut—he wouldn't and didn't know what to do with the truth. Yep, she'd been right.

"So how are we going to work this out?" Cole's deep voice cut through her thoughts, his rugged yet handsome face dappled in moonlight and shadows.

"You mean my working for you? Or my living here with a colicky baby?"

He nodded, his laser gaze, noticeable even in the dim light, nearly making her squirm. "Part A."

Under the sweater, she shifted Flora to the other breast and waited until she latched on. "Well, while you were at the hospital I had a long talk with Gretchen. She seems to have an unfulfilled grandmotherly gene. She said she'd be happy to take care of Flora when I work."

"Maybe you should just work part-time at first."

She wanted to yell, *Don't you get it? I'm broke. I need the money!* But she swallowed another sip of tea instead. "But you hired me to work full-time. I want to keep my side of the bargain."

He went quiet again and studied his expensive brand-name shoes. The man oozed wealth. And good looks. "I'm glad to pay you the amount Trevor agreed on, but maybe at first you can come in half days or something."

"You do realize that women only get six weeks' maternity leave in the US and return to work all the time, right? I'm that single mother in med school who never missed an overnight shift, and my only support system was other med students. I graduated the same day as everyone else with my baby swaddled in a sling across my chest. People do what they've got to do, you know? Gretchen said she's happy to help. Let me do what you hired me for, okay?"

Take that!

"That's commendable. I'll give you that." He remained thoughtful, probably analyzing her plea, seeing right through her, figuring out how desperate she was. "I suspect Dad will be in the hospital at least a week, and then be sent to rehab after that. Once he comes home, though, Gretchen will have her hands full caring for him."

"You've got a point, but by then I can find other child-care arrangements." *Keep positive even against the odds. You've got to.*

He thought for a moment or two. "Reasonable enough." *Whew!* He put down his teacup and slapped his big palms on his thighs. "Well, I'll leave you and Flora to your feeding. It's been a long day."

She nodded. "I can hardly keep my eyes open."

Before he left the room, she studied his huge silhouette in the doorway, broad shoulders, long torso, big in every way, a man's man. Fine-looking man. Yet he'd been gentle with Flora. Was it totally wrong to find your new employer sexy? Yet she couldn't deny she did.

"May I ask you a question?" It had been bothering her since she'd noticed the identical scars on his forehead when she'd first met him, and to be honest she needed something to get her mind off how attracted she was to him.

He turned. The epitome of patience...and gentleman cowboy...sexy.

"Did you have a broken neck?"

The hallway light cut across his profile. He scrunched up his face, obviously surprised by her comment. "Another astute observation, Dr. Silva. I take it my halo-brace scars tipped you off?"

She nodded, trying not to look smug, though definitely feeling it.

"When I was fifteen I was riding a bucking bronco, got bucked off and fractured C1-C2. I was fortunate not to have a spinal-cord injury, as you can obviously tell." He held out his arms, palms up, looking over his own body.

"No need for fusion?"

"Three months wearing that brace did the trick. It also changed my life goal of becoming a rodeo star." He smiled and deep vertical grooves cut through his cheeks. Yeah, that was sexy, too.

But his confession made her laugh outright. "A rodeo star?"

"You're looking at Cattleman Bluff's former junior rodeo bucking-bronco champion." He said the mouthful with an amused twinkle in his eyes, as if the title might have carried some clout around here at one time.

But rodeo stars were as foreign as extraterrestrials to a girl from Boston. "I'd say I was impressed, if I had a clue what that meant." If this was her idea of flirting, she wasn't doing a very good job.

His closed-lip smile widened slowly, finally revealing a fine line of teeth, and the effect, combined with the lingering glint in his eyes, sent a shiver through her. *Oh, man, this could be bad. Dr. Montgomery is gorgeous.*

She swallowed. "I'm sure you were a regular star around these parts." She tried out her version of cowboy talk, her accent no doubt falling far short of the mark. *These pahts.* Come to think of it, she could imagine him in dungarees and a torso-hugging cowboy shirt. And what she'd give to see the man wearing a cowboy hat.

"Easy come, easy go," he said.

"Sounds pretty ouchy to me."

"That, too. I guess you can say I'm a doctor today because of that accident."

"Weird how life goes sometimes, isn't it?"

"Yeah." He gave her statement some thought. "Well, I hope you both get a good night's sleep."

"Thank you." She imagined sympathy in his eyes, and, though she didn't want his pity, she appreciated his caring on some level. These days she didn't have anyone in her corner, with the exception of Dr. Rivers, and he was far away.

"I also want you to know that, if it hadn't been for you, my father might have been a hell of a lot worse off. You haven't even begun to work in the clinic, and you've already impressed me."

He'd paid her a compliment, and this from a man who didn't seem to do heartfelt. It made her beam. "Thanks. I hardly know your dad, but I like him. He's got a lot of spunk."

"Yeah. He's probably too stubborn to die, but the thought of dealing with his aphasia, well, let's just say, we'll all be miserable. I'm hoping his symptoms will resolve quickly."

"Me, too."

"Well, like I said, thanks to your fast thinking. Good night." With that he turned and headed in the opposite direction from her bedroom wing. She watched him for a while, thinking that for a big man he moved with grace, and she definitely liked his style.

Flora had fallen asleep. Lizzie rose gently, hoping not to wake her, and started toward her room. It had been a crazy first-day meeting at the Montgomery ranch. How was she supposed to know there was a wedding going on? And a stroke? Sure was one hell of a way to break the ice with the family, though.

Cole seemed more city slicker than rancher, but thanks to his taking the time to talk with her she'd gotten a glimpse of his inner cowboy, which had probably shaped the man he'd become. The thing that really mixed her up, though, was she really, really liked what she'd seen.

CHAPTER FOUR

COLE WAS TOO keyed-up to sleep. Worries about his father had peaked a few hours back when he'd been assured by the attending physician that Tiberius Montgomery was stable. He'd sat by his father's hospital bedside and watched him sleep for an hour or so after that, then decided, as the doctor had said, that it would be okay to go home. He thought about going to his own apartment in Laramie to sleep and be nearby, but decided to head back out to the ranch because of Elisabete.

The last thing he'd expected was to step in on a tired and frazzled woman walking the floors of the living room doing her best to calm a wailing baby. Her nearly black hair had been set free from the earlier braid, and thick tendrils had covered her shoulders. The contrast with her creamy skin had been unnerving. Then in the kitchen he'd noticed the tiny sexy mole above her upper lip, and had nearly fallen off his chair, which wouldn't have been a good thing considering he'd been holding her baby.

She had the potential to be an incredibly beautiful woman, yet did little to enhance it, and still had managed to make him sit up and take notice. When was the last time that had happened? Maybe that was the special factor about naturally attractive women: sometimes they didn't know it, and that made them all the more appealing. Or maybe it was just her youth.

Not a good thing for their situation, and, he had to be honest, with her fresh out of medical school, he'd be doing a lot of teaching at the clinic.

He sat on his bed, scrubbed a hand over his face, tired to the core, yet restless just the same, and accepted the fact that peace of mind wasn't in his immediate future. He had a father to rehab, a new-to-him medical clinic to run, a diamond-in-the-rough doctor to train, not to mention an innocent baby who deserved a good start in life to look after. And why should he feel even partly responsible for that, too? Because any decent man understood innocence deserved protection.

He shook his head, then lay back on his pillow. And to think all he'd expected to do when he came home was run his brother's medical clinic and keep up with his father's accounting books. Simple, right? He laughed wryly to himself. Since when had life ever played out the way he'd expected?

Good thing he intended to spend the entire day Sunday working the ranch with a couple of Jack's cowhands, then in the afternoon he'd go to the hospital to check in on his father. It would give Lizzie and Gretchen time to bond with the baby, and hard work had always been the best way Cole knew to run away when his personal life got out of control.

Hell, that was how he'd decided to take a fellowship and train for transcatheter heart-valve replacement. He'd chosen to learn the minimally invasive mitral-valve replacement procedure when hardly anyone in the country had heard of it, rather than deal with his mother's death. He hadn't spent more than two days consoling his father after the funeral. He just hadn't been able to take the emotional strain seeing his dad fall apart like that. And leaving early as he'd done, as always, he'd left another burden on Trevor's shoulders.

He rolled over. *Sleep, where are you hiding?*

Lizzie took extra care after nursing Flora Monday morning. She fought back tears when she diapered and dressed the precious baby in one of the few terry-cloth onesies she owned. "Everything's going to be fine today, Flora bear. I promise. Gretchen is a sweet lady who'll take good care of you."

The baby watched Lizzie as she talked, as if trying to understand. Such intelligent blue eyes. She knew her mother's voice, too, and the thought made the brimming tears spill over Lizzie's lids. How was she going to survive today?

I've got to work. "Everything I do is for us." She kissed her daughter's chubby cheek and inhaled her special baby scent, savoring it. Not wanting to let go.

She'd had to leave Flora with so many different people when she'd first been born in order to keep up with medical-school classes and clinics. Then the toughest job in her life: the addiction center. It'd about ripped out her heart to leave her, too, but she'd had to graduate if she wanted to pass the boards and get a job. And she needed an income to pay the rent. At least now, in Wyoming, she'd only have one sweet grandmotherly type watching Flora every day, and she'd see her baby every night and all day on the weekends.

Quality time was what mattered, she repeated over and over to help dry her tears. Squeezing her baby close, she forced a smile, pulled back and put on her brave face, not wanting to leave Flora seeing her cry. "Are you going to be a good girl for Gretchen?"

A gurgle and coo answered her question.

"I love you so much!"

* * *

Lizzie kissed Flora goodbye in Gretchen's arms. Cole could have sworn he saw her eyes well up, yet like a trooper she pulled herself together and didn't utter a word about missing her baby on the drive in to work. Though frequent sighs and constantly fidgeting hands in her lap gave her away.

His back was stiff from hard labor yesterday, walking the range, sinking posts, but it was the kind of ache that did a man good. But the pain wasn't distraction enough to keep him from noticing how Lizzie had pulled her hair back in that braid again and wore silver hoop earrings large enough for shooting practice. Even though she'd chosen a long-sleeved white tailored shirt with dark slacks, sending a clear unisex message, he couldn't help but notice what seemed to be all woman beneath the wrapper. Yeah, this couldn't be good.

"How's your dad doing?" She broke into his spiraling sexual thoughts.

"Pretty well. He's recovering his strength quickly, which, as you know, is always a good thing with CVAs. Fingers crossed his speech will turn around, too. Another day or two of observation, and they may even skip sending him to rehab if he continues on this trajectory. The doctor said a home occupational-health worker and speech-recovery therapist may be all he needs."

"That's fantastic. Wow, we dodged the bullet there, didn't we?"

He liked how she'd already thrown herself into the center of his family using *we* as if she were one of them. "Yes, *we* did. Keep sending good thoughts for his speech. You know how recovery can change day to day in the hospital."

"Yes, and I certainly will."

It got quiet then, as if the early morning drive had been their routine for years. She sighed and glanced out the window; he snuck a peak at her intently watching the scenery. He'd forgotten how amazing the Wyoming landscape was, how the sparkling blue sky over this big box-shaped state accentuated the brown and golden shades of strata on the low-lying hills, and made the prairie grass look like one huge shaggy carpet.

"How're we gonna work this today?" she asked, checking back in, one foot suddenly tapping a quick rhythm on the floor of the car. He didn't peg her as someone to get nervous about a new job, though she did seem to run on adrenaline and nerves.

"The patients?"

"Yeah, are you willing to let me work on my own unless I need your help?"

"I'd like to supervise, if you don't mind."

She started to protest.

"At first," he said to appease her, but mostly to shut her up because he didn't feel like debating the topic. He was the senior doctor and she might as well get used to it. "Then we can evaluate the situation and go from there."

"I guess that's reasonable."

"You didn't think I'd just cut you loose, did you?"

She tossed him a teasing smile. "A girl can hope."

"Charlotte, the RN, is going to triage the appointments. Give the more complicated patients to me, and maternal/child to you. Oh, and I'll take all of the cardiology patients. Obviously."

"How sexist is that?"

"It's not sexist if it's practical. I know squat about maternal child health, and I figure, since you recently had a baby, not to mention the fact that you've just graduated from medical school and most likely studied the topic more recently than I have, you're more suited to the job." *Not to mention that you're a woman. Okay, so it did sound sexist. It was beside the point.*

She shook her head, but moved on, apparently deciding not to argue. Good choice. "I'd like to do as many procedures as possible."

"Fine with me. I'm spoiled by having a team of nurses do my dirty work."

"See, you are sexist and since when do cardiologists ever get dirty?"

"Who's being sexist now? There are plenty of male nurses."

She smiled, clearly liking the verbal sparring. "Point taken. But I don't think of cardiology as a profession that gets dirty."

"You've heard of angioplasty, right?"

"You do those?"

"I do, and I take it a step further, I replace mitral valves, too."

"But that's open-heart surgery."

"Not the way we do it these days. I use the same route as angiograms. TAVR or TAVI—have you heard of that?"

She turned her head toward him, disbelief in her eyes. "You do transcatheter aortic-valve replacements?"

"Also known as trans-catheter aortic-valve implantations. Yes—" he sounded smug and couldn't help it "—that would be me."

"Oh, my gosh." Except it sounded like *ohmahgosh*. "You're, like, a star in medicine!" Except it sounded like *stah*.

"You've heard of me?"

"You're, like, the god of cardiology. I can't believe I didn't add that up." She tapped her hands on her knees. "Wow. I'm working with a genius!"

"I wouldn't go that far."

"Oh, I would. You launched a whole new minimally invasive approach to mitral-valve replacement. No major incisions, the heart doesn't have to be stopped or put on bypass, there's quicker recovery time. We learned all about that in my fourth-year cardiology module. This is freaking amazing."

"Hold on, it's not like I created it. All I did was hear about a great new product, and ask to be trained by the medical-device company. Granted, I was one of the first in the country to do that. Okay, the first." He tried his best not to look too proud. "You know the old saying with medicine: watch-one-do-one-teach-one. Now I travel the country doing in-services training for other doctors. Spreading the word. Kind of like a TAVR evangelist." He enjoyed her gushing, but went the humble route anyway. "I'm just a teacher."

"The procedure sure has changed a lot of lives for the better. It probably doesn't cost nearly as much as the old way of doing things either."

"Well, the surgery isn't for everyone, but, yeah, it has helped a lot of people."

He pulled into the parking lot, which put an end to the conversation. When they got out of the car, he thought he noticed a fresh blush on her face, and she looked at him differently than when they'd left the ranch. Okay, so now he knew she was the kind of woman who was impressed with what a man could do, not only his appearance, which was a definite plus for him. Yet there was that link to a man's abilities again, rather than the person. Yeah, but that was all beside the point, because nothing was going to happen between them.

Why did he need to remind himself?

She walked ahead, as if she couldn't get inside the clinic fast enough. There was a spring in her step, and when she looked over her shoulder at him she displayed a giddy grin. "I can't wait to actually start practicing medicine as a real doctor. Finally!"

Doctah!

Oh, good grief. Why didn't she just click her heels and declare to the world *I heart medicine*? He refrained from rolling his eyes, not wanting to dash her rookie excitement.

"Charlotte, our RN, is going to give us a tour of the clinic before we get started," he said.

"Makes sense. We don't want to spend the day looking for things, right?"

So far he liked her logical way of seeing things.

As they approached the clinic door he reminded himself Elisabete Silva was only twenty-six years old, fourteen years younger than him. A different generation, a millennial. His job was to refine, educate and send her out into the world of medicine as a better all-around doctor.

That was all.

So why did he keep checking out the natural side effects of that bouncy walk of hers? Because he was a man, and, unless he was dead, it was what a man did.

Inside the clinic, after general introductions—Cole had met the head nurse at the wedding on Saturday—Charlotte lifted one silver brow above an obvious appraising stare. "Well, I hope you know how to work hard, because there's no room for slackers in this clinic."

Ah, a tight-ship lady. Hmm, Trev had left off that part. Was that a subtle threat to Cole, too? "Don't worry, Lotte." He used her preferred name, since Trevor had already filled him in. "We'll all pull our load. I know Trevor is a tough act to follow, but I'm older and wiser." He liked to think he was anyway. He winked.

Lotte softened her stern expression at the mention of Trevor. Or maybe it was the wink. "You'll do fine. All you Montgomery men are overachievers." At least she was free with her compliments. "It's just the new one I'm worried about."

Uh-oh, Lotte played dirty, landing a sucker punch below the belt. Did she not know Lizzie was standing right there? He glanced at Lizzie, expecting to see insult, but she wore an amused smile, keeping her true reaction to herself. Good call. But what he'd give to know what was running through her head.

"If it's all the same, I'll look after Dr. Silva," Cole said. "I'm sure we'll all get along just fine."

By the expressions on both women's faces, he wasn't the least bit sure about his prediction.

"Now, how about that tour of the clinic?" he said.

Midmorning, their routine was sliding into place. Granted, Lotte had only allowed half the usual appointments for the next couple of days, but between Cole and Lizzie they were tearing up the house, if he did say so himself.

He sat in Trevor's office, inputting the necessary computer data on his last patient; Lizzie tapped on the opened door. He glanced up, and the vision of youth and eagerness changed his serious outlook to something more in the carefree department. The woman was contagious.

"I've got a patient who doesn't want to take birth-control pills. She doesn't want the implant or the shot. I've talked her into using an IUD."

"Okay?" *And what does this have to do with me?*

"You said I had to run everything by you."

"Oh, right. Yes. So can you do what she wants?"

"I've only inserted a couple of them." She'd lowered her voice to a whisper.

"Do we even have intrauterine devices in the clinic?" he whispered back, playing along. Since when had playful been a part of his clinical routine?

"Charlotte says we do, and she's willing to assist me. That okay with you?"

"It'll have to be, because I don't know the first thing about placing an IUD birth-control device. Should I have whispered that?"

That got a broad smile out of her, a reward far greater than he could have imagined. "Okay, great." She charged off, like an athlete getting called into the game.

"Let me know how it turns out," he said, but suspected she didn't hear him since she was already back in the patient-exam room with the door closed.

Twenty minutes later, Lizzie emerged from the room with a victorious smile on her face. Cole watched in amusement. Lotte followed behind. "You did fine," the nurse said, matter-of-fact.

"Thanks!"

Shortly afterward the patient stepped outside the door, dressed and ready to leave. Lotte started to give instructions, but Lizzie cut her off, taking full responsibility for her patient. The nurse's disgruntled expression didn't go unnoticed by Cole.

"Remember you may feel mild cramps like you're getting your period for the next couple of days. That's normal. But if you have excessive cramping or begin moderate to heavy bleeding, come back and see me right away."

"I promise." The young woman stepped closer to Lizzie. "Dr. Silva, thank you so much for helping me choose a method of birth control that doesn't involve hormones, shots or pills."

"I'm glad we found something that works for you, Gina."

When the patient exited the hallway, Lizzie scrunched up her face, raised her shoulders, fisted and shook her hands in a super-happy gesture. "She called me 'doctor.'"

Cole shook his head just before he went in to see his next patient, though, for the record, he thought her enthusiasm and excitement over the job were cute, even if they did tick off the RN.

During lunch she locked herself in Julie's office, the one she'd taken over. He stood outside and listened, positive some crying was going on in there. Wow, she hadn't given the hint of being homesick for her baby, yet he couldn't deny the sound of crying. He was about to knock to invite her along to the café in town, thinking it might make her feel better, when Lotte informed him that Lizzie was expressing. Expressing what? Then he heard some weird mechanical noises start up inside.

Feeling the urge to put fingers in his ears, he strode out of the building to buy some lunch, trying his damnedest to put the image of a woman pumping her breasts with a machine out of his head.

"TMI, Charlotte. TMI," he called just before he closed the back clinic door.

Lizzie couldn't believe how great the day in clinic had gone so far. Then it hit her: she hadn't thought about Flora for, what, an hour? Her chest clinched and her eyes immediately stung. More proof she was a terrible mother. Flora's sweet face appeared in her mind's eye and she ached to cuddle her. But she'd just finished a pre-summer-camp physical for a ten-year-old boy, which he'd passed with flying colors, and she was printing out a copy for his mother to turn in to the camp nurse when Cole snagged her in the hallway.

"I've got something for you to hear," he said.

"Okay, just let me give this to my patient's mother and I'll be right there." She'd called Gretchen during lunch, and she'd promised everything was going great with her baby, so she'd focused back on work. But, oh, how she missed Flora whenever she came to mind.

Once she'd finished her appointment she went directly to Examination Room Two, where she'd seen Cole step back inside. Still feeling guilty over letting Flora slip out of her mind from time to time, she forced those thoughts away and knocked before entering. Tomorrow she'd bring a picture of her baby and put it on her desk.

"Mr. Harrison, this is Dr. Silva. I wanted to have her listen to your heart, if you don't mind."

"Not at all, Doc," the skinny older man said. He sat on the examination table topless, having removed the worn and faded clinic exam gown.

"Dr. Silva." She loved hearing him call her that. "I was doing a routine physical and, since it is rare to hear all four heart sounds on auscultation, I thought I'd share it with you. The fact that Mr. Harrison is thin helps a lot. Have a listen."

He'd said the sounds were something to share, but she knew it was a test. He didn't just want to share heart sounds with her, there had to be something more going on, and her hunch was it would be up to her to find the reason.

She pulled her top-of-the-line stethoscope from around her shoulders. It had been a gift from Dr. Rivers when she'd graduated near the top in her class. She put the ear tips in and placed the bell on the man's chest in the first of the five positions for listening to heart sounds. True, most of the time doctors and nurses only heard the *lub-dub* sounds, but, seeing as this was an over-sixty and thin male, all four sounds were in fact fairly loud and clear, a rarity. She listened again, more carefully, then heard the faint click between S1 and S2. A murmur. Mitral-valve regurgitation.

"How long have you had mitral prolapse, Mr. Harrison?" She skimmed her gaze over Cole before giving the patient her undivided attention, and she'd seen it, the pleased glint in his eyes and the slight nod of the head. Yes, she'd heard exactly what he'd pulled her in here for.

"What's that?" the man said.

Cole stepped in. "Normally Mr. Harrison doesn't visit the doctor unless he has to, but since he turned sixty-five his wife insisted he have a physical. He's never been diagnosed with mitral prolapse, and seems to be symptom-free, but we'll do a cardiac workup, get a twelve-lead EKG and send him to a specialist for an echocardiogram, then decide how best to treat him."

She nodded in agreement, then, realizing the test was over and she'd passed, she said goodbye to the patient and Cole and went back to work. She still had three more patients to see before the clinic closed. One would be a pelvic exam and Pap smear, another a follow-up for asthma and the last a surgery follow-up for gallbladder removal—a clinic schedule just like a real doctor.

Lizzie loved doing this job. It was the one thing in her life she was sure of…she'd been meant to be a doctor.

On the way home she talked Cole's ear off, but couldn't help herself, because she was bursting with excitement and needed to share it with someone. Plus, she was on her way home to see Flora. What more perfect way to end a day than that? When she got this way, all worked up and happy, she talked way too fast and slipped into her strongest Boston accent, and Cole probably couldn't understand half of what she was saying, but she couldn't stop. Unlucky Cole was the guy sharing the car with her, so she talked and talked and talked. Poor man had to listen to her full-speed-ahead monologue almost the entire ride home.

As her day wound down, and her breasts tightened with milk, she could barely wait to see her daughter. Thoughts of helpless and beautiful little Flora washed over her, making her want to instantly hold her. She'd missed her daughter, of course she had, yet the breather, doing something she also loved, had been a welcome relief from nonstop child care. What an awful thought! Her face screwed up in confusion, and she needed to either break down and cry or talk about it. Sobbing in front of Cole after her first day at work was not an option. "Is it wrong that I enjoyed being away from Flora today?" she said, her chin quivering.

"Are you asking me if you should feel guilty?" He took his eyes from the road and glanced at her.

She nodded, without a shred of confidence in what his answer would be.

He hesitated, obviously searching for the best words. "I wouldn't dare judge, but I suspect it's normal for any mother to want a break. Nothing to feel guilty about. It's got to be stressful as hell to be totally responsible for another life."

How could this man who'd never been a father nail her exact feelings? "Yes. Very."

"And your being away for a few hours has probably done both of you some good."

"You think? You know, I never heard from Gretchen this afternoon and I'd asked her to call with any questions, or if Flora got too colicky, so that's a good sign, right?"

It was his turn to nod. "Believe me, if Gretchen needed to contact you, she would have."

Swimming on a stream of insecurity, she couldn't help herself. "So you don't think I'm a horrible mother?"

"Not at all. Plus, I think you are a fine doctor in the making who gives her patients a hundred percent of her attention. Which they deserve."

Insecurities duly banished, she sat straighter, her eyes wide and heart warmed from the compliment. "You think?"

"I know." He smiled and that Wyoming cowboy grin nearly knocked the breath out of her. This man was downright dreamy when he smiled.

"Thank you!"

He looked relieved when they got to the ranch. When Gretchen appeared at the back door with Flora in her arms, a rush of motherly emotions flooded every pore, and all Lizzie wanted to do was rush to her baby and hold her. To kiss her and make sure the little one knew her mother was back, and they'd be together the rest of the night. From the distance of the car, she studied her precious one, the face she swore had changed since just that morning, and beamed with love. Her daughter was the icing on the cake of her first dream day on the job and she started to rush toward her.

But Cole pulled her back by the arm, first.

"I couldn't get a word in edgewise on the drive home, but I just wanted to tell you that I think you were outstanding today. You carried your load and you've got a lot of potential and I'm going to see to it that you turn into that top-notch doctor you obviously want to be."

This was the wildest compliment she'd ever gotten, and being that her confidence had been lagging lately, she was so grateful he'd said it. One moment she couldn't find a placement in a resident's program, and the next she was impressing one of the finest cardiologists in the country. How crazy was that? Enthusiasm riding on adrenaline spilled over and coursed through her veins, it pumped into her head and washed her brain in happy juice, further proving she'd made the right decision to come to Wyoming. She couldn't control herself.

She popped up on her toes and threw her arms around Cole's neck for a tight hug. "Thank you so much." Then without thinking she pulled her face out of the crook of his neck and kissed his cheek, complete with end-of-day stubble. "Thank you, thank you, thank you," she said, staring into a pair of startled light brown eyes.

Afraid to linger too long, getting lost in his sexy gaze, she rushed off toward Gretchen. Riding another flood of thanks, she took her precious baby into her arms, kissed Flora's chubby cheek, cuddled her close and thought this had been one of the best days of her entire life. Thanks to Cole Montgomery and the kind surrogate grandmother. Then, getting walloped with a sudden surge of how much she'd missed her daughter all day, she burst into tears.

CHAPTER FIVE

BY FRIDAY, COLE WAS worried how Lizzie would survive. He'd heard the baby crying in the still house in the middle of the night, most nights. He'd witnessed the dark smudges beneath her eyes worsening each new morning. Because of his ongoing neck issues he preferred to stand at the nurses'-station torso-high counter to do his charting in the clinic, and he'd had to step in more than once to ease the friction developing between Lotte and Lizzie. Both were strong-willed women, and wanting the best for the patient; their outspoken styles often clashed. Tension had built all week and something needed to change.

As they drove to the clinic Friday morning he glanced at Lizzie, who'd closed her eyes for the duration of the ride. Her thick hair pulled back tight into the usual braid, the same silver hoops in her ears, the white tailored shirt and black slacks that had turned out to be her personal uniform—perhaps that was the extent of her wardrobe?— her long, delicate fingers twitching lightly from time to time as she stole a few last moments of rest.

He needed to step up as her employer, to guide her and offer gentle advice on how best to serve her patients along with the medical staff. She was a ball of hyperinsecurity one moment and suffered from overconfidence the next, was edgy yet overly sensitive, and she'd been driving the head nurse crazy. That couldn't continue. He'd let her rest for now, but once they arrived at the clinic he'd invite her into his office for a friendly chat.

She made a quiet snort waking herself, then sat straighter and, with bleary, though still sensational eyes, glanced at Cole. "Sorry."

"For what?"

"I think I snored." She rubbed her makeup-less eyes and stretched minimally under the confines of the seat belt.

He smiled, not wanting to make her self-conscious. So he lied.

"I didn't hear anything."

"Oh, good, then."

But, since he'd lost sleep over it, he did need to broach the subject foremost on his mind. "Listen," he said. "I've been thinking we should start having weekly meetings at the clinic. You know, to talk about our patients and share information. As your senior staff person, I should mentor you and as the newest doctor, you can share your discoveries with me, too. What do you say?"

"I've been running everything by you at work." She looked doubtful, like a person realizing they're being set up.

"Yes, but we rarely have time to discuss anything in depth. If you were a resident you'd have daily rounds with fellow doctors and senior staff, you'd be questioned and tested on all the medical possibilities, given assignments, and questioned again. I owe it to you."

She inhaled slowly. "I don't know how we'd squeeze that in at work, though. There's hardly time to breathe, and when I take lunch I need to express for Flora." Without warning she broke into tears, the mark of a stressed-to-the-limit person.

Cole was at a loss for what to say or do, so he let her cry until she recovered a modicum of composure.

"I'm sorry," she said. "I had no idea how hard both working and taking care of my baby would be. How do mothers do it? I think I'm losing my milk." She bit her lower lip, fighting back emotion.

He didn't have a clue how to comment on that at first other than to say, "I'm sorry," but then decided to go the scientific route. "I'm pretty sure science has proven that machines can duplicate most human functions, but they don't ever come close to replacing the soul of the matter." Idea fresh in his mind, he touched the handless smartphone connection on the steering wheel, desperately needing female backup. "Call Gretchen," he recited.

Within seconds he heard her voice. "Hello, Cole, is everything okay?"

"Gretchen, can you bring Flora to the clinic around eleven-thirty today?"

"Sure. Is there a problem?"

"No problem. Just make sure she's hungry when you leave." He hung up and looked at a clearly flabbergasted Lizzie. "From now on you can nurse your baby during lunch. I'll have a big healthy meal delivered in every day, and you and Flora can have some bonding time on the job."

"You don't have to…"

"Of course I do. It's my job to keep you from melting down. You're here to help me, not to become my next patient."

"I'm sorry."

"Nonsense, no apologies needed." He needed to hit the right tone with his explanation, not make her feel guilty or coddled. "This is purely selfish on my part, so I'm being practical. You need to be a high-functioning member of my staff. You've been doing a commendable job under the circumstances, but there's always room for improvement, right?"

She dutifully nodded, a side of Lizzie he hadn't seen before. Then it occurred to him that there was more to say; there were more ways he could help her, since they lived under the same roof. "Furthermore, if Flora wakes you more than once a night, I'll expect you to come and get me. Not that I can nurse her or anything, but I can walk a floor just as well as you, I suspect. We can share the insomnia between us, then it won't be so bad. And if that helps my new doctor look more alive and keeps her head about her on the job, then I'm happy to do it."

The grateful expression on her perfectly lovely face was hard to resist, but he kept his eyes on the road after a brief peek. He'd never once offered to help with Eddie, Victoria's five-year-old son. Probably because the kid couldn't stand him, and to be honest the feeling was, well, mutual. Victoria had overindulged him and the boy thought he was the center of the universe. But a three-month-old baby like Flora needed to feel cared for and soothed.

"I can't ask you to lose sleep, too," she said.

"You're not asking me anything. I'm telling you our plan to get both of us through the next few weeks. Men are task oriented, in case you hadn't noticed. That's all."

"You're serious, aren't you?"

"You bet I am. Oh, and while I'm on a roll here, let's make those staff meetings back at the ranch." He'd been going to the hospital to visit his father every night after work, but Gretchen had kept him informed about a few things back home. "You've been having dinner in your room, and that's fine for now, but since my father is doing so well, he might be coming home soon. They've agreed to send daily home-health caregivers for the initial week, Gretchen has agreed to sleep over for the first couple of weeks, and we'll see how it goes from there. But my point is, once he's home, we should all take dinner together. He'd want it that way, and, out of respect for him, it's the least we can do. And that includes you. Then after dinner you and I can retire to the library to discuss medical business."

"What about Flora?"

He'd expected a huge protest, but got a maternal-minded question instead, which proved she was a better mother than she gave herself credit for.

"Bring her with. Or let Gretchen bathe her and put her to bed. You figure that out. Bottom line, we need to get on with the job of making you the best resident material out there so you won't sit out another moment from your medical career."

He figured putting it that way she couldn't possibly argue with him.

"Okay. Thanks. I'm in." Amazingly his plan had worked. "Let's make this a miniresident program. Teach me everything you can. It's the best thing for me and the baby, and hopefully your father will benefit from the family dinners as much as I will. Now I know I made the right decision coming here." She beamed.

Cole smiled at the road, thinking his crazy plan had actually worked. Then a chill slipped down his spine at the implications—Lizzie Silva was about to become a part of what was left of his family. Was he ready for that?

At least it was only for the next few weeks. If growing up and surviving medical school, residency and two fellowships had taught him anything, it was to take each huge project one single step after another, never looking at the big overwhelming picture, but concentrating on every small achievement along the way. The days and weeks would click off quickly over the next few weeks, and soon his job would be over with Lizzie. If he worked it right, she'd find a resident placement. She and Flora would pack up and leave once Trevor and Julie returned home, and his life would finally get back to how it was supposed to be.

Traveling. Teaching. Working hard. Uncomplicated by personal relationships.

Alone.

He pulled into the clinic parking lot wondering what in the hell he'd just accomplished, and, since he hadn't a clue, he screwed up his face in confusion. Why did he suddenly feel he was getting the short end of the stick in this clever plan?

Thirty minutes later, after seeing her first patient of the day, Lizzie appeared at Cole's office door.

"I've got a question." She stood smack in the middle of the frame, neither stepping inside nor remaining in the hallway, her stethoscope draped like a shawl over her shoulders, dark hair pulled into a ponytail and piled high on her head.

"Okay, shoot." He stopped typing his notes on the laptop to give his undivided attention, and it never took much for him to give Lizzie Silva all of his attention. Basically, all she had to do was show up and, *boom*, he was all eyes and ears.

"Mrs. Ruth Overmoe is in my exam room complaining of ongoing bloating and nausea unrelieved with over-the-counter gas and acid medicine for a few weeks now. I have a hunch it's more than that. She mentioned today's weight was a few pounds more than usual and attributed that to the bloating. No dietary changes. No history of heart disease. What do you think about my running a CHF workup on her?"

"Are her ankles swollen?"

"Not much, and she says they've been that way for years. The belly bloating is the new issue."

"Any signs of JVD?"

"Nope, her jugular veins don't look distended."

"What do you propose for the workup?" It was a test, yes, but he needed to make sure she didn't miss any labs or other tests that might be useful to make an initial diagnosis.

"CBC, lytes, UA, BUN, FBS, EKG."

"Don't forget liver-function tests and get a chest X-ray."

"Yes, that's a given. Too soon for natriuretic peptide levels?"

"Let's see what we find first with these studies," he said. As she thought, her lips puckered and smoothed, stealing his undivided attention, nearly making him lose his medical train of thought.

"Got it." She smiled and turned to leave.

"Good find," he said, pleased with her level head and solid medical background. From over her shoulder, as she walked away, she flashed him a wide smile, one that reeked of confidence and pride. "I'll expect a full report on congestive heart-failure symptoms exclusive to women at our first meeting."

"You got it," she said without turning around, unfazed by his challenge.

Cole wasn't sure how helpful these after-dinner sessions would be for Lizzie, but, as for him, he definitely looked forward to them.

"Here's your girl," Gretchen said, making her daily clinic entrance exactly at 11:30 a.m. in Lizzie's office the following Friday morning.

"Thank you!" Excited to see Flora, Lizzie reached out and took her baby into her arms. In one short week, it had quickly become the highlight of her work day. Whether sensing her mother or smelling milk was nearby, the child opened her eyes, squirmed and soon fussed. "Oh, honey, I miss you so much." She kissed her baby's cheek, which was growing chubbier by the day, and cuddled her close to her body. "Mommy loves you."

Gretchen had been nothing short of a godsend these past couple of weeks. She glanced up at the older woman in deep appreciation. "You know, since you started giving her the evening bath she has really settled down at night. It seems her colic may have passed."

"I have a little trick I remember from when I had my babies. Not that they've given me any grandbabies to try it out on or anything, but that's an issue for another day." Gretchen gave Lizzie her pretend disgusted expression. Having chatted a lot since arriving at Circle M Ranch, Lizzie had learned how much the woman longed for grandchildren, but neither of her daughters were married. "I use an old rubber water bottle filled with warm water and lay it across her tummy after her bath. Then, when I put her down, I give her a pacifier to suck on."

"That's a great idea, and it certainly helps Flora settle down faster," Lizzie said as she unbuttoned her blouse and opened the nursing-bra flap, then watched with delight as Flora nuzzled close to nurse.

"I think she senses you're settling down, too."

"What do you mean?"

"You've come a long way since arriving at the ranch. You were one edgy and nervous lady at first. Now we've all gotten into a comfortable routine, and Flora must sense it. Babies love routines."

"You may have a point."

"Well, the test will be this Sunday when Tiberius comes home. If anything can disrupt the peace, he will."

"Have you been to see him?" Flora was eagerly nursing, and, though it was always great to have alone time with her, today Lizzie chose to use the time to quiz Gretchen.

"A couple of times. He's doing really well, gets most sentences out the way he wants, but once in a while he can't quite express himself, and it bugs the holy hell out of him." Gretchen's eyes widened. "Oh, pardon me for cussing in front of the baby."

"I don't think she noticed." Lizzie grinned, thinking how terrible she'd been the first few weeks alone with her colicky baby. Not that she'd cussed *at* her precious one, no, but she'd been so exhausted and frazzled that she'd been short with a lot of people, some who had even been trying to help her. And sometimes, feeling under a pressure cooker, she'd revert to cussing a blue streak like when she'd been a rebellious teenager. Realizing those days seemed to be behind her, or maybe it mostly had to do with nursing Flora, but whatever the reason, she completely relaxed and slipped into the moment. Life was good. For now. Two weeks ago it had been like living a nightmare in Boston with zero prospects, staying in that dark and tiny single-room apartment after quitting that horrible job.

Now she had a new job and a great place to live, she enjoyed her work and the one-on-one mentoring time with her boss, and she owed it all to the big handsome Wyoming hunk, Cole.

"I'll leave you two alone now," Gretchen said, tiptoeing toward the door. "Be back at twelve-thirty."

"Thank you," Lizzie said, glancing at her contented baby then making a blanket statement for everything good in her life in the right here and now, kind of like saying grace and meaning it with all of her heart. "I can't thank you enough," she whispered, and closed her eyes.

By the end of Lizzie's second week at Circle M, Cole realized that Lizzie hadn't knocked on his door once in the middle of the night. Could bringing Flora for midday nursing have helped fine-tune the baby's schedule? He shook his head no. He'd taken the time to read up on colic in babies and knew that, though the problem still remained mostly a mystery, the biggest help turned out to be time. Sometime around three or four months, except for extreme cases, the colic issue seemed to cure itself. Whether it was a baby's metabolism finally figuring things out, or all the mother's efforts to avoid spicy foods and caffeine paying off—whatever the reason, or maybe for no reason at all—sometimes the problem simply disappeared.

He put his hands behind his head and turned out the bedside lamp, then closed his eyes. Instead of letting himself fall asleep, he remembered Lizzie's luscious expressions earlier as she'd listened while he went over the day's list of patients and quizzed her on each one. Thinking of her inquisitive green eyes, and how her mouth pouted slightly while she thought, assured he wouldn't find sleep in his near future. Crying baby or no crying baby, Flora wasn't the source of his insomnia. His father's health wasn't either. Or the huge cardiac conference he was missing in NYC this weekend, nor was the running of the Cattleman Bluff Medical Clinic with its outdated computer hardware. No. The source of his insomnia was simple to identify—Lizzie Silva.

CHAPTER SIX

COLE BROUGHT TIBERIUS home Sunday midafternoon, and Lizzie stood in the entryway. She waited for him to come through the door while wearing Flora in a front-facing baby carrier, the child's current favorite place to watch the world. Plus it was an online tip as another way to help decrease colic in babies.

The older man begrudgingly used his quad cane to stabilize himself as he made the trek from the parked car to the porch. His wild mane looked whiter than she'd remembered, but someone, most likely his nurse, had done battle with it and his hair lay somewhat flat against his head. Cole was directly behind him watching his every step. He obviously played down the fact he was within catching distance in case his father lost his footing or anything. Tiberius would throw a fit if he caught on, so he stayed a foot or two back and allowed his father to be independent. Once they crossed the wide porch, Cole shot ahead to open the front door for him.

"I can do it," Tiberius said, grumpily. "I'm not an invalid." Then quietly he muttered, "Yet."

"Just trying to be helpful, Dad." For that comment, Cole received an impatient squint, and Lizzie ached for him. "Gretchen, have you got something for Dad to eat?"

"Blasted hospital food is worse than airplane food."

More grumbling from Mr. Cheerful. Then he noticed Lizzie and Flora, and his irritated expression softened a little. "Well, look who's still here. I thought you'd have high-tailed it back to Boston by now." He walked toward her, and she was about to answer him, but Mr. Montgomery hung a left before she could think of a good comeback—which was unusual for her—heading for his chair in the living room. She suspected he recognized a kindred spirit in her, one blustery phony to another. At least that was how she saw him, all bark yet tenderhearted. With Tiberius clearly in a sassy mood, she followed his lead.

"You can't get rid of me that easily, Mr. Montgomery." Lizzie understood the best way to deal with a grump was to be grumpy right back. "You've inherited us for another four weeks, so just get used to it." She followed him, and beat him to his chair, then puffed the pillow tucked into the corner of the arm rest. He sat, hanging on to his annoyed expression, but he couldn't fool her, because, like a thin veil, right behind the grouchy gaze was a "happy to see you, too" glint.

"Weren't you the one who saved my life?"

She sputtered a laugh. "Hardly. We all did our part, and you turned out to be stubborn enough not to let anything too bad happen anyway."

He sat with a thud. "How do you know me so well?"

"Maybe you're the grandfather I never had." Which set a whole other connotation into place—but the last thing she'd ever think of Cole as was a father, not with the way she'd already developed a crush on him. True, he was fourteen years older than her; she'd done the math. They'd grown up in different generations, he was a Gen X and she was a Gen Y—a millennial. She didn't write letters or listen to voice mail. She didn't know what the world was like before computers took over. Their taste in music had to be light years different. But sometimes she fantasized about him.

Realistically, besides practicing medicine, what did they have in common? Yet, each day she felt more drawn to him because of his calm, his maturity, his knowledge… not to mention his excellent looks and how he was sexy without even realizing it. She especially liked that. She sighed as she repositioned the pillow exactly where Tiberius pointed behind his back, forcing her thoughts back on track.

"No, thanks. I've already got a grandson. James is enough."

"Now you're just hurting my feelings," she said.

"Didn't mean to do that." The sincerity in his eyes nearly bowled her over. "I'm still cranky from being stuck in the hospital for a couple of weeks. Torture. Pure torture."

"Can I get you anything?" she said, a sudden puddle of compassion.

At that moment, Gretchen appeared in the doorway with a tray of food in her hands. Cole rushed to find and open a TV tray to set it on. With three people and a baby circling his favorite chair, Tiberius protested. "Back off, folks, I'm not going to croak today or any day this week. Give me some breathing room, would you?"

Watching to make sure he had use of both hands, without residual weakness on the right, Lizzie stepped back and passed a sheepish glance at Cole. He raised his dark brows in warning, obviously implying, *Be prepared—you ain't seen nothin' yet.* She liked passing secret messages with Cole, especially since it meant she got to look into those handsomely wise eyes.

"I think I'll take Flora for a walk," she said, heeding his warning, deciding to leave Tiberius to Cole and Gretchen. Besides, it was a beautiful warm and sunny afternoon, and if she timed it right she could make it all the way out to the ash and maple-tree grove with the pond before Flora's next nursing was due. She could sit in the shade in privacy and enjoy Wyoming's big sky and abundant nature, and feeding her baby all at once. Which reminded her she was hungry, too. She bent her knees, since bending at the waist was impossible with the baby carrier, and snatched half of Tiberius's roast beef and cheddar cheese sandwich. "Mind if we share?" She passed him a mischievous look, raised her brows, and, when she had his full attention, took a big bite before he could utter a word.

The corner of his wrinkled mouth lifted in a near smile. "Wouldn't want to rob a woman of nourishment. But don't even think about touching that gingerbread cookie."

"Not even half?" she said, her mouth filled with wheat-bread sandwich.

"Don't push it, girlie-girl." He feigned a grouchy glance, and she gave him a genuine smile, because she really liked the old guy, and she suspected he liked her just as much. Then, with the smile lingering on her lips, her gaze settled on Cole, who watched the odd interaction between his father and the newest boarder at the ranch. A tiny hiss and sizzle snaked down her chest as she walked out of the living room and into the great outdoors where the sun warmed all of her, not just the hot, fluttering part planted there by Cole.

Later, after nursing Flora and dozing off to sleep for a few minutes, Lizzie wandered back to the ranch and the stables. She'd already figured out that Flora loved to see the big horses.

"You ever want to take a ride, just let me know." Cole surprised her from behind.

She turned away from petting the big reddish-brown

horse. "I've never been on a horse, wouldn't know what to do."

"I'd be happy to teach you. All you have to do is ask." Their gazes met and held firm, and she wondered if he'd just offered something more than horseback-riding lessons. Nah, she'd probably read too much into that super-sexy gaze.

"If Gretchen's hands weren't full with your father, I might take you up on it right now."

One brow curved toward the other. "Good point. Any thoughts on how she's going to be able to watch Flora and my dad?"

Lizzie inhaled and let her air out slowly. Fortunately, she'd given this topic lots of thought. "I'm one step ahead of you, Cole. Remember Gina, the woman I helped with birth control?"

He nodded, looking so darn much like a real cowboy she thought she'd traveled back in time.

"Well, she and I have been keeping in touch, and it turns out she has two kids under three. She could use some extra money and when you mentioned your dad was coming home, I asked if she'd consider watching Flora. She'd love to, even said she'd bring her by for midday nursing."

"That's great. I'm glad you're making friends."

She tossed her glance upwards. "Too bad Lotte and I can't be friends, too."

A benevolent smile coursed his mouth. "She's what we call a crusty old nurse. Got a lot of opinions and isn't afraid to push them on everyone."

"Someone needs to tell her she's a little outdated because she won't listen to me."

Suddenly losing the sexy cowboy gaze and taking on a diplomatic expression, he squared his shoulders. "Well, you do have a way of pushing the limit, in case you're not aware of it."

She shook her head. "Look, I know I'm not exactly an ambassador of goodwill, but I'm the one fresh out of medical school. When did she get her RN license? Thirty years ago?"

Cole walked to the horse Flora was watching while she cooed and squealed, and patted its cheek. The horse blew hot breath through flared nostrils in appreciation and the sound drew another shriek from the baby. "She's a wealth of experience that you could tap into. Being fresh out of school can sometimes be a disadvantage, you know?" he said, admiring the horse rather than look at Lizzie. "You might just learn from her if you give her a chance."

She'd honestly never considered Lotte a wealth of information, but seeing the sincerity in Cole's avoiding eyes, and more so in his demeanor, she realized he'd just used a velvet hammer to call her out. Maybe her head was bigger than her knowledge? "Is this where I'm supposed to eat humble pie?"

Instead of seeming frustrated, he grinned. "I remember being full of myself, too. Just ask my dad—he'll tell you story after story. The thing is, a lot of the old ways still work just fine. You might learn some time-saving tricks if you give Lotte a chance."

"And no one, including you, likes a know-it-all, right?" How had she gotten called to the vice principal's office in a stable? And more important, why did she have the strong desire to change immediately? Couldn't he see her overconfidence was just a ploy to cover her insecurity?

He dipped his head and studied his boots, maybe a little disconcerted by her usual full-speed-ahead approach, then sent her a narrowed gaze. "If you're here in Cattleman Bluff to learn, I'm suggesting you find every opportunity available. Nurses are a great source of practical knowledge and it never hurts to make them allies."

He turned to leave, and partly because what he'd said

made perfect sense, plus the fact he looked like a real-life cowboy in those tight jeans and that button-up shirt, except without a hat, she couldn't let him go just yet. "Thanks," she said. "I get it." Really she did. She needed to soften up around Lotte. She waited for him to turn, expecting a surprised expression, but she found so much more. His eyes examined her as if he'd just seen her for the first time. Couldn't the man see how she felt about him? His extra attention sent a shiver up her neck. "Um, Flora's due for a nap—any chance I can take you up on that horseback-riding lesson offer?"

"The old man's taking a nap, too, and Gretchen's watching over him like a mother hen. No reason she can't look in on Flora, too. Let's do it."

Excited over the prospect of taking her first ride, she rushed to Cole, popped up onto her toes and bussed his scratchy cheek, thinking he'd put her in her place without humiliating her and now he was kind enough to take her horseback riding for the first time in her life. This guy was too good to be true. "See you soon." When she pulled her head back, the flash of fire in his dark eyes sent more hiss and sizzle slicing through her, except this time it sank deeper. She couldn't very well stand there locked in his sight, not when Flora's little hands flapped like a hummingbird, so she turned and headed out of the stable. As she strode toward the house, she realized she was out of breath and it had nothing to do with walking or carrying Flora.

Cole refused to be a cliché, damn it—boss falling for his attractive employee. But he stood there, watching her walk away, enjoying every sway of her hips and the bounce of her dark hair, and liking the way it made him feel alive in a way he'd forgotten lately. This was crazy.

And it had to stop.

He started to saddle O'Reilly, the Irish pony from Connemara, dark brown with calico markings on her legs, for himself—his father had brought her over five years ago for the ranch—thinking Trevor's aging buckskin Appaloosa, Zebulon, would be good for Lizzie. He relaxed and enjoyed the process of saddling the horses, not having to think, just mindlessly following the steps. He should let go and see what the afternoon would bring, think of it as nothing more than a relaxing ride with a lovely lady. What harm could that do? Then tomorrow, back at the clinic, he'd go back to business as usual. Because he couldn't let his growing attraction to Lizzie interfere with what was best for her. Best for both of them.

Thirty minutes later, Lizzie showed up in jeans and tennis shoes—better than flip-flops anyway—obviously eager, though nervously chewing her lower lip. That expression alone nearly stopped him dead in his tracks. He really needed to quit focusing on her mouth.

"Ready?" he said, going into forced casual mode. The horses were saddled and waiting.

"As ready as I'll ever be."

He couldn't stand there staring at how cute she looked, so he moved in, weaving his fingers, making a footrest for her to launch off. "Put your left foot here and swing your right leg over Zebulon's back."

For once, she didn't resist, but followed instruction to the T.

"Now slip your feet into the stirrups, so I can adjust them. You can hold on to the horn for now." He shortened the stirrups to fit the length of her legs. "How's that feel?"

"About right, I guess." She looked all around stiff and anxious, and he tried to remember how he'd felt the first time he'd sat on a horse. But he'd been way too young to remember all the details now. Come to think of it, he kind of had grown up on a horse.

Not wanting to prolong her worries, he handed her the reins. "Hold these gently, no need to pull them. When you want Zebulon to walk, just squeeze your inner thighs right here." He patted the area just behind the horse's girth. "When you want to stop him lean back a touch and pull back on the reins. Not too hard, though—he'll get the message." He stroked Zebulon's neck and kept talking. "Just don't do too many things all at once 'cause that will confuse him and he'll ignore you. Oh, and horses prefer gentle voices."

Her eyes were large, concerned-looking and maybe a little panicked.

"Don't worry," he said. "Zebbie's gonna follow O'Reilly, and we'll take it easy for your first time. Okay?"

She nodded, still looking uncertain, an expression he'd rarely seen on her.

"I'm not gonna let anything happen to you, Lizzie, so relax. Zebulon will pick up on your nervousness and he's known to be stubborn. You don't want to set off his stubborn button."

"Okay." Her nostrils flared slightly when she said it, and Cole understood the city slicker felt completely out of her element, so he grinned warmly to help soothe her.

"You're going to do fine," he said in his gentlest voice, as if he were talking to a spooked horse.

"If you say so." She sounded breathy, and he liked it. A lot. He gave her a quick lesson on how to turn the horse right and left, and let her practice a time or two with him right there in case anything got fouled up.

Once he'd mounted O'Reilly, they set off at a measured pace until he sensed Lizzie was settling in. "See that ridge way out there?"

She followed his direction and narrowed her eyes. "Yes."

"From there you can see the entire ranch. Feel like giving it a try?"

Obviously hiding her nerves, she gave a courageous firm nod, and he admired her for that. But he admired her for a lot of things, and not all of them strictly physical. This woman had a lot to offer, and some guy down the road would be lucky to have her. "Let's go." Not him. "Remember, whenever you want Zebulon to go, squeeze your thighs together. If he doesn't respond right off, squeeze a little tighter."

She suddenly shared a shaky yet beaming smile with him. "No wonder women like to ride horses."

He laughed—now that was the lady he was used to—and led out, wondering how it might feel to have Lizzie Silva squeeze her thighs around his hips. Oh, damn, he wasn't going to be a cliché. *Don't forget.*

The clear sky left the sun alone to bake their backs as they rode at a trot toward the trail to the ridge. "How you doin'?" he called back.

"Surprisingly well. This is fun."

He turned to look at her and was rewarded with her happy expression along with a lightly flushed complexion. Yeah, he didn't know one person worth their salt who didn't enjoy riding horses. With one last glance and smile, he switched back and led the way to the ascending trail.

"What's up with you and your dad?"

Whatever peace and tranquility he'd gathered up so far on this ride vaporized as chaotic memories broke in. "What do you mean?"

"There's some major tension between you two. Am I right?"

He hated when people saw right through him, especially when he'd worked so hard to cover it up. "We have some old business, I guess you could say, like everyone."

"It seems pretty current to me."

Was it her street smarts or her training as a doctor that had her zeroing in on the situation? "Well, if you want to focus on the current issues, he's getting old and neither Trevor nor I want to take over the ranch."

"It's his legacy, right?"

"Yup. Key word being *his*, not mine or Trev's."

"He's worked hard to build it."

"That he has. I think he holds me responsible for Trevor following me into medical school. I was the firstborn and it was taken for granted I'd take over someday, maybe build an empire for the Montgomery name—best steer in the country. You know how that goes."

"Not really. Foster care, remember?"

"Oh, right, I'm sorry. So you probably fall on the ungrateful-son side with my dad, then, right?"

"No judgment from me."

He decided to leave it at that, since he hadn't figured out how to bring up the subject with his dad and didn't think a woman who'd never had a dad could be empathetic. Things were complicated. He'd made a great career for himself yet his father still thought of him as a runner. "I've used my career to avoid dealing with him."

"You don't come home much?"

"Not since my mother died."

"I can kinda tell he still loves and misses her. Probably why he likes to play grumps all the time."

"I didn't hold up my end of the bargain. Never did. Tried to impress a girl and fell off a bucking bronco, broke my neck. Then got it in my head I wanted to be a doctor, not a rancher. Then, to make matters worse, Trevor followed my lead. My mom used to keep me and Dad from killing each other when I was a teenager. Theoretically speaking. After my neck, I went the academic route when all Dad wanted was more help with the steer. He wanted to teach me everything he knew, didn't give a crap about my winning the county scholastic decathlon three years running. Mom put her foot down when he refused to pay for college."

"Wait a second. You broke your neck for a girl?" That low and husky laugh tumbled out, and, realizing the absurdity of his story, he laughed with her.

"Yup. 'Cause that's how I roll. At fifteen anyway."

She laughed until Zebulon protested, then covered her mouth and pushed the last of her chuckles back down her throat. What else was there to say after that? He'd been involved with Victoria for almost two years and had never told her about why he'd broken his neck. Now all he did was take a short horseback ride with Lizzie and spill his guts. He squinted toward the sun, inhaled more fresh air, deciding to chalk it up to the great outdoors and the woman with the green eyes that drove him wild.

Twenty minutes later, with only the creaking of their saddles and the plodding of the horses' hooves, his lungs filled with crisp air and mind with earned solitude, they'd made it to the ridge.

"Let's take a break here." He dismounted, and led O'Reilly to some grass, then started for Zebulon, who'd taken it upon himself to share that patch of prairie grass with O'Reilly and had already moved closer. "Whoa," he said gently, stopping the horse long enough to allow Lizzie to swing over her leg. He grabbed her from behind by the upper hips and helped her down the rest of the way, liking the weight of her in his hands and the heat simmering from her body.

How many times did he have to tell himself reacting to her like that was crazy?

She turned quickly in his arms, cheeks flushed from brisk air, mood clearly exhilarated from the ride. "That was incredible. I loved it."

She'd taken right to riding, and discovering she loved

it set off a light, flighty sensation in his chest. "I thought you might."

"Wow!" She'd skipped right past their warm moment that evidently he was the only one feeling, trading him in for the view, but not before he zeroed in on that sexy little mole by her upper lip. "Would you look at that?"

He'd rather look at her, but he followed her invitation toward the cliff. The entire Circle M Ranch sprawled out before them, neatly divided into sections of green and brown grazing land for their steer, separate grazing areas for the horses, perimeter and pasture fencing protecting the cattle from the roads, and irrigated areas where they grew much of their own hay and grains to help feed the steer. Even all the way up here, he could smell the hay. From this angle the view was impressive, even though he'd seen it hundreds of times.

The prairie grass had turned light brown due to summer, covering the rolling hills and flatlands dotted with greener shrubs and trees. Their home was dwarfed by the panoramic view. It was the first time he'd been up here since coming home, and the view, as always, caused a swell of pride in his chest. His father had taken a dream and made it come true. Truth was, Cole wanted to impress her with the Circle M Ranch and all it stood for, to give her a clue how sacred this land was to his father. After their earlier conversation, it was also a lesson for him.

Unless he or Trevor stepped in, their family ranch might be gone in a matter of years. Or the *M* would be torn down and replaced by someone else's initial. He didn't want to dig into those consequences right now, not with Lizzie by his side, but the realization helped him understand better his father's frustration.

"I don't think I've ever breathed fresher air," Lizzie said, breaking into his thoughts. A light breeze had kicked up and loose ends of her hair, though mostly pulled back into a ponytail, flicked and tickled around her face.

"Welcome to our little bit of heaven on earth."

"I can't imagine what it's like to grow up in a place like this."

"I'll be honest, I took it for granted. Now that I live in Baltimore half the time and Laramie the rest, I appreciate the peace and solitude when I visit."

"Which isn't that often, right?"

"Don't ruin my moment." Something about Lizzie made it easy to say exactly what he thought without worrying it would be taken wrong—another exact opposite from Victoria.

"You ever think about moving back?"

He raised his head, taken aback by her comment. Did he? "Let's just say sometimes I wonder what will happen if I don't."

"You think you could live all the way out here and continue to be cutting-edge in cardiology?"

And there was the rub.

"Another good question that I don't have an answer to." She'd managed to make him edgy, even while gazing at the cattle kingdom his father had staked out for himself and his family. He had a lot of thinking to do on the subject, especially now with his father growing more frail by the year, hell, by the month.

He really didn't want to think about that right now, though, not with the tall, intriguing woman standing so near, sharing the view with him. He'd much rather be close enough to smell her shampoo and to see the tiny golden flecks he'd just recently noticed in her soft hazel-green eyes. That tiny mole. Or to think about, for instance, how it would feel to put his hand on her waist.

She must have sensed his thoughts because she turned toward him, pushing hair out of her eyes as she did, smiling and practically willing him to come closer. He took a step or two and she met him halfway. They reached for each other as if they'd planned this lovers' getaway for weeks. What was going on? He didn't care; he pulled her into his arms as she stepped closer and soon his desire to sniff her hair and nuzzle her long neck became reality.

They stayed there, hugging, getting used to the feel of each other, and him liking every little discovery. Like how she fit so well against him; her being tall meant he didn't have to hunch over, which took a lot of discomfort away from his neck. Her head fit neatly beneath his chin, and sharing the view with her made him want to fly. So much of what Lizzie Silva did was disturbing to his equilibrium, yet uplifting, too. He wondered what he did for her, and worried it fell far short of what she managed to bring out in him.

He needed to shut down his brain, to quit overthinking every little thing, because all of these thoughts were stealing from their moments together. Lizzie was normally like a skittish colt, yet right now she snuggled into his chest, relaxed and calm; he couldn't let this slip by. Soon, though, her head moved from under his chin. He looked downward to her questioning gaze, and without a second thought, he answered her by pressing his mouth to hers. Their lips settled together in a warm and exhilarating seal. Hers were soft and smooth, and he swore he caught the scent of vanilla and tasted it from her lip gloss.

Though knowing this was exactly the opposite of what he should be doing if he didn't want to be a cliché, he deepened their kiss. She obliged, opening her lips enough for him to touch the tip of her tongue and then to discover the velvety-smooth inner side of her mouth. He tasted hints of peppermint even as he inhaled that vanilla gloss.

Being a man, he knew exactly two gears, On and Off, and right now On took control. His hands wandered down her surprisingly fragile back and then lower to her hips, enjoying all that he grabbed on to. He was vaguely aware of her arms tightening around his neck when he did. She'd heated up the kiss, canting her head, probing and delving deeper with her tongue, and the entire front of his body tensed in anticipation of what might come next.

With blood rushing through his veins from her being so close, he didn't stand a chance she wouldn't notice his natural reaction. But he didn't care. She'd started it. She was a doctor, knew all about physiology. He just wanted to keep kissing her and feeling her. And she seemed to want the same, kissing harder as her hands kneaded and rubbed his neck and shoulders.

Minutes passed as their kisses danced and whirled into a passionate knot. He tasted and breathed her, and made it very clear that she'd turned him on. The problem was, there was nowhere to go from here. Sure, some heady kisses were great, but, really, he knew this had to end. She'd been brought on board to help at the clinic, and he hoped to help her, too. She wasn't meant to be a playmate.

She was a new mother, for crying out loud—what was he doing working her all up when reality screamed that this wasn't supposed to happen? He *was* a cliché.

Then he felt it. His guy switch turned to Off.

Yeah, they couldn't keep this up. Not now.

Not ever?

His hands lightened their grip on her hips. He removed his lips from hers as he drew back. With regret he looked into her eyes and saw the hesitant disappointment there, and for that he was glad, because he was definitely disappointed, and didn't want to be the only one. At least he hadn't thrown himself at her; every part of this make-out session had been mutual. Beyond a doubt.

But what the hell had they just done except complicate things?

"Must be all that fresh air, huh?" She broke the stretching silence, answering his unvoiced question.

Sure, they could always blame it on the weather.

He glanced sheepishly at her. "Yeah. I hope I—"

"Please don't apologize, because then I'll have to, too, and, to be honest, I really liked kissing you."

Since she put it that way… "Me, too, but we have no business dragging sex in to this situation."

Her eyes shifted downward beneath her full, arched brows. "Then we should probably ride back now."

Damn, he'd hit a nerve or something and now she wanted nothing more to do with him. He didn't want to force the subject of sex or no sex, so he agreed. He ran one feather-light knuckle over her smooth cheek regretfully. "Okay, let's go, then."

Cole barely needed to help Lizzie mount her horse this time around, and before he got on O'Reilly she'd already turned Zebulon around, heading back toward the trail.

He'd let his most honest feelings loose just now, and all it had done was confuse things. That couldn't and wouldn't happen again. Because he was damned if he would be a cliché.

Lizzie rode down the trail in silence. She'd let down her defenses and kissed Cole. What a stupid idea. Cole had reprimanded her about dragging sex in to their situation, and she really should have known better. Men these days got called out for inappropriate behavior with employees and slapped with lawsuits all the time. For all he knew she might have been setting him up. Wasn't that how Dave had felt after going out with her for six months, then finding out she'd gotten pregnant? The last thing she'd needed was a baby while going through medical school—how could Dave possibly think she'd gotten pregnant on purpose? Yet he did. The fact that her schedule had been crazy and she'd messed up on the birth-control pills had never entered his mind. Nope, he'd flipped out and roughed her up to make his point, too.

A powerful man like Cole couldn't be cautious enough, and she'd just allowed something as simple as a horseback ride on the ranch let her make a bad choice. Of course Dr. Cole Montgomery was off-limits, and the fact she'd thrown her arms around him and kissed him as if they were on a date proved she was suffering from new-mom brain.

Seriously, what had she been thinking?

That he was the sexiest man she'd ever met. That there was something special about him and his family. That she'd give anything in the world to belong to someone like that, to be a part of it and for Flora to have a man in her life like Cole.

When they got back to the stables, she dismounted without his help, didn't want him to have to touch her again since he'd backed off pretty quickly after they'd kissed. Was it something she'd done? When their gazes slipped over each other's, she sent him a secret message—*Don't worry, Doc, it won't ever happen again*— then headed back to the house, pretending she needed to rush back to her baby.

Sunday dinner was mandatory. Dad was home, cranky and restless. Gretchen had cooked his favorite meal of prime Montgomery beef stew with root vegetables even though it was summer, had baked corn bread and made cold cucumber salad. Cole wanted to avoid Lizzie, but wouldn't dare stand up his father for dinner—especially since he'd made such a big deal out of it to Lizzie—and definitely not on his father's first night home.

They gathered at the huge heirloom table, big enough to seat twenty people, seeming sadly lacking as a party of four and a half—that was if Lizzie and Flora showed up. Maybe it was time to start eating in the kitchen. Ah, what was he thinking? That would never fly with his traditionalist father, especially not on Sunday nights.

The moment Lizzie walked in to the room, things brightened. A little buzz zipped through Cole, reminding him of earlier, making him wonder if she'd replayed those moments as many times as he had in the few short hours since they'd shared those kisses. Or had she thought of it at all?

Their eyes met and held briefly, and something told him she'd already taken his words to heart—*we have no business dragging sex in to this situation.* It didn't matter if they liked kissing each other or not, they'd messed with their work dynamics and it would take a while to get over that. At least for him, because, as he'd already established, he *was* a sad cliché.

Yet he still had to sit across from her at the table and couldn't very well avoid looking at her.

She'd pulled her hair back and put it in a loose roll on the top of her head, wore bright pink lip gloss and a dark blue short-sleeved blouse. Her eyes stood out as always, and her gentle smile of greeting made them turn upward at the edges. It suited her.

In such a short time he'd already gotten accustomed to her face, to seeing her every day, which was a very bad thing. He frowned and she must have taken it personally by the flash of confusion in her gaze as she pulled it away and settled on his dad, instead.

"Mr. Montgomery, you're looking dashing tonight," she said, even though his father wore a faded plaid shirt, with an obvious stain on the yellowing crew-necked undershirt.

"Call me Monty, like all of my friends, and cut the crap." He shook out his napkin, signaling it was time to eat.

Lizzie laughed good-naturedly, something else he liked

about her, adjusting Flora in the wraparound sling she wore across her torso. "Okay, Monty, I feel honored to be considered a friend."

Monty fretted, as if he'd already regretted opening the door to friendship with her. "Pass the stew, would you?" he barked gruffly.

Cole stood and carried the large ceramic tureen to his father, lifted the lid and let him serve himself even though it took more effort than usual, then walked around the table and held it for Lizzie to dish out hers. Just because he'd kissed her like a randy teenager earlier didn't mean he'd forgotten how to be a gentleman. He figured things were awkward because he was sending mixed-up messages, and she focused on the food rather than look at him. He wanted to kick himself for kissing her—uh, no, honestly, he didn't, but right now he hated the repercussions—because it fouled up their working relationship. She had so much to learn and he wanted to help her.

"Gretchen, this smells fantastic," Lizzie said.

Gretchen dutifully brushed away the compliment. "Oh, I've been making this for the Montgomerys for years."

"Best food I ever had since coming here. You're a great cook."

"Oh, not really." Cole had made it over to Gretchen and let her serve herself. "Thank you, Cole."

"She's right," he said. "I've been away so long I'd almost forgotten." She patted his hand in appreciation once she'd filled her bowl.

Cole sat to the right of his father and served himself. The corn bread got passed around and after his father's terse grace they all dug in.

"I'm not really used to eating family-style." Lizzie wasn't afraid to break the silence, and Cole was glad about that.

"Families don't eat together in Boston?" Monty plunged ahead without a second thought.

"Didn't have a family. I was mostly in foster care." She spread butter on her corn bread. "I never really felt part of those families."

That stopped Monty cold. He quit chewing and stared at Lizzie, obviously trying to decide how to put his other foot in his mouth, too. "Now, that's a cryin' shame." He shoved another bite into his mouth, deep in thought.

"I had my grandmother until I was ten. Loved her to bits. But she died and it wasn't until I was fifteen when I met Janie Tuttle."

Cole didn't want his father to make any more lame comments so he spoke up. "Was she a foster parent, too?"

Lizzie glanced appreciatively at him, knowing she'd already shared a part of her history with him. "Yes. She's the reason I got scholarships to college and she put the notion in my head that I could be a doctor if I wanted to be."

Achy warmth clung to his chest, making him wish everyone could have a solid home as he and his brother had growing up. "She must have been a great lady."

"She was an old spinster school teacher, didn't have a clue how to handle a teenager, but she took a chance on me. I guess I had the good sense—well, after being in a whole lot of not-so-great foster homes—to appreciate her interest in my education. She died my second year in medical school, but at least she knew I'd made it there." She blinked away the moisture that had gathered and made her eyes look large and dewy.

The achy warmth increased and clinched like a vise. He forced his gaze to his food to give her space to recover, if that was what she wanted to do. Lizzie had lost everyone who ever cared about her; now all she had was Flora. The last thing she needed to feel was that she had been taken advantage of by him. Sometimes life really didn't seem fair.

"You're an inspiration," Gretchen said. "You've made yourself a success."

Lizzie laughed lightly. "Hardly. After I'm through here I don't have a job."

He didn't think for half a second before the words popped out of his mouth. "I'm going to do something about that."

Her full, arched brows lifted a good inch. "How are you going to do that?"

"I'm going to get you an interview with the head of the internal-medicine resident program of your choice." He was? "I'm going to coach you and help you present yourself in the best light and I will guarantee you make a great impression."

"My choice? You have that much clout?"

Probably not, but he'd work out the details later. "The key is you can't pick the same hospitals you just tried to get into. Come up with your secondary list. Give me five choices, and I'll get you in."

"You'd do that for me?"

He wanted to. "Yes." Maybe partly to get her out of his life, or partly to impress her? Oh, hell, he wasn't sure why he wanted to do this, but he did. That was the important thing. He wanted to help Lizzie and Flora. He liked them, cared about them. In order for them to have a good life, she needed a resident placement. Hmm, he'd make some calls this week to see if any spots were left open in any of the east-coast programs. "Are you willing to consider a list of programs I compile for you, too?"

"How can I say no to that?" She offered a somewhat disbelieving grin, and Cole knew he'd have to prove to her that he was a man of his word. That he could be trusted. And their kissing had nothing to do with this.

He took a bite of beef, wondering one thing. Was he the kind of man who could be trusted?

Soon after Lizzie had finished eating, Flora got squirmy and fussy. "I'm so sorry but I'm going to have to take care of her." She looked earnestly at Gretchen. "I really wanted to help with the dishes, too."

"Don't bat one eyelash over that. Go take care of our sweet baby."

Looking relieved, she glanced over at Tiberius. "It's great having you home again. If there's anything I can do, please let me know."

Cole could tell his father, slowed by the latest TIA, was searching for some witty comeback. "Thank you, I've got all the help I need," he finally said. "Take care of the little one." Or maybe finding out about Lizzie's childhood helped him bite his usual acerbic tongue.

Cole didn't have a clue what age babies sat up, but it seemed that sling thing wouldn't be the best way to hold Flora much longer. All anyone could see was the top of her head at the dining table and that shock of dark flyaway hair. It made him smile. But he kind of liked seeing her face and those inquisitive baby eyes, so awed by everything. So intelligent in a totally innocent way. Since he had some free time that night, he got it into his head to do some extra research. Truth was, Lizzie wasn't the only one to have gotten under his skin.

CHAPTER SEVEN

Monday morning, Cole and Lizzie agreed to travel to work in separate cars, since she had to deliver Flora to the new child care. He'd gotten the okay and loaned her his father's car, and was grateful not to be stuck in the same car since things had gotten awkward between them the rest of Sunday after their kiss. He lingered on at home and enjoyed an extra cup of coffee while making a quick online order before leaving, then listened to the weekend sports wrap-up on the radio for the ride in to work.

He'd no sooner walked in to the clinic when Lotte rushed him with laser-like tension in her eyes, and with Lizzie right behind her. His first worry was that they'd had another argument and he wasn't sure if he was ready to be diplomatic yet or not. *Work it out yourselves, ladies.*

"Been a horrible accident out at the Waltons' ranch," Lotte said. "One of the cowhands got butted and gored. You'd better get out there."

Cole glanced at Lizzie with alarm. When was the last time he'd worked the ER? "Ever see that in your big-city ER?"

"No, but I certainly saw my share of stab wounds. A deep puncture is a deep puncture, right?"

"You're probably right." Trauma medicine was far from his specialty, but he'd been raised on the ranch, had seen all kinds of injuries related to spooked cattle. He could at least help until the ambulance arrived. If he recalled right, his father had told them the Waltons were raising buffalo now.

"Where's the trauma kit?" she said.

"Good question."

"This way," Lotte said.

They set off for the procedure room where the trauma and delivery bags were kept, right on Lotte's heels.

"Everything you should need is in there."

Lizzie grabbed and opened it, and did a quick inventory.

"I'll call an ambulance and have Rita cancel the morning appointments," Lotte said. "If anyone shows up, if they want to stick around, we can try to squeeze them in the afternoon."

"Sounds good." He gathered extra gloves and gowns, since there might be a lot of blood involved, even though his biggest fear was internal injury from the patient getting rammed by a bison. "Let's go."

"This should be all we'll need until the paramedics get there," Lizzie said, closing the bag and looking calmer than Cole felt.

On the drive over, to keep his mind occupied, he quizzed her on deep-puncture-wound care and signs and symptoms of internal bleeding. As always, she aced it.

Fifteen minutes later while they were still in the car, a young cowboy on horseback led them to the corral where the man was down. They parked and rushed to the scene. Hell, it was Mike Walton; they'd gone to school together. The guy had been working the ranch all his life, which proved you never knew what might set off a steer, or, in this case, a bison.

The cowhand chattered every step of the way, filling them in on the particulars. "We was moving them through the chute, this guy was the last one. Something must have spooked him and set him off."

Cole found Mike in the corner of the corral on his side, moaning.

"The damn thing hooked him with his horn after he rammed him into the post. Just picked him up and threw him back down like he was tumbleweed or somethin'."

Cole knew that big animals found comfort in groups and got nervous when they were alone. Any number of things could have set off that bison. He figured they'd spent their time and manpower energy getting the bison out of the corral after that, and probably hadn't looked after Mike at all. He dropped to his knees.

"Mike, you with me?"

Mike moaned and opened his eyes. "Hurts like hell. He gored my ass." He lifted his head a little while he talked, which was a good sign his upper spine was okay.

One thing Cole understood for sure was if a person had to get gored, the buttocks were by far the best place. Lots of padding and minimal nerves ran through the area, unless he'd been gored deep enough to hit the obturator nerve—then there could be a lot of damage. "Can you move your leg or foot?"

Mike tested out moving his foot. It worked well enough, another good sign.

"This is Dr. Silva. She's going to help me."

Lizzie nodded hello, then didn't waste a second. She grabbed large bandage scissors from the ER kit to cut off the jeans. "We need to get a better look, okay?" she asked, but only after she'd sheered through most of one pants leg.

Mike gave a tense nod with thick dust in his hair and mud smudges all over his face. His cowboy hat lay trampled a couple feet away. "Pardon my derriere, ma'am."

"Not a problem."

"So the bison butted you with his head before he gored

you?" Cole asked, engaging him in conversation just to keep Mike focused, and so he'd feel like he was doing something.

Mike gingerly moved his hand over his abdomen. "Knocked me against the post and I fell on my face. Couldn't breathe. Then he gored my ass."

Lizzie stopped cutting long enough to see where Mike gestured. "You in pain in the stomach area?"

Mike nodded again. "A little, but my butt hurts like hell."

Cole knew cowboys often had high pain thresholds. There was no telling what a little meant. Also, the fact he could talk in sentences was a good sign that one of his ribs hadn't punctured his lungs. "I'm going to get rid of your shirt so we can see anything obvious, okay?"

Another stoic nod.

He popped the buttons on his shirt and opened the front; the guy was already bruising. "Check this out," Cole said to Lizzie.

She gently pressed around the area. "The good news is the area doesn't feel hard or stiff." Though Mike definitely flinched when she touched him. "I'm going to take your blood pressure. See where we stand." She motioned for Cole to pick up where she'd left off with cutting off the jeans and took over the examination.

While he did battle on sturdy denim with the bandage scissors, going up the back of Mike's leg, she checked his vital signs. Fortunately the BP was in normal range, maybe a little high from the pain, and his pulse wasn't quick or thready according to Lizzie. Mike might have been tossed around by a bison, but maybe he'd survived without rupturing his spleen or a kidney.

Cole finished cutting off the jeans and they saw the baseball-sized puncture wound on Mike's right buttock. Blood trickled out from the angrily torn edges of flesh.

"We'll have to leave the deep cleaning and debridement for the hospital, but we can at least go ahead and clean and bandage the wound for now," she said and went right to work. "The hospital can do computerized tomography to look for any intra-abdominal or retroperitoneal hemorrhage or organ damage."

Cole understood the ER would need to assess damage to his pelvis and hip, and his respect for Dr. Silva was growing leaps and bounds.

"You'll need surgery to debride the wound."

"How long will I be off work?"

Cole knew Mike had a ranch to run, but the healing would take as long as the puncture needed to fill in with new granulation tissue. The process of secondary intention worked from the inside out.

"That's hard to say," Lizzie spoke up. "Let's just concentrate on getting you to the hospital for now and see what happens after that, okay?"

Once discharged, they'd see him in the clinic for follow-up care. Eventually, knowing Mike, he'd be the guy at the bar with a great ass-injury story, and if anyone doubted, all he'd have to do was drop his trousers. The odd thought put a smile on Cole's face, but mostly what made him smile was the expert way Lizzie handled the situation, making him feel like nothing more than a supervisor. She had everything it took to be a fantastic doctor. All she needed was a little more polishing and general experience.

Soon the ambulance pulled into the long drive and Mike got transferred onto a gurney, and while Lizzie gave her report to the paramedic, Cole called ahead to the hospital and gave a thorough rundown of the event to the emergency-intake doctor. While he did, it occurred to him what a great team they'd made, he and Lizzie. By ten o'clock they headed back to the clinic, and, since

Lizzie had taken over at the scene, he felt compelled to do a little teaching.

"Steer, cows and bison have eyes on the sides of their heads so they can see almost three hundred degrees. They can graze and watch for predators at the same time," he said.

"No, *suh*!"

"Pardon?" Must be one of those Boston idioms?

"Really? That's so cool. If we had three-hundred-degree vision, we wouldn't have any blind spots when we drove." She showed some interest, and, as usual, added her unique take on the subject.

Being in that corral had brought back a truckload of memories, and since he'd felt fairly useless back at the scene, he went on. Granted, the information would only be of use if Lizzie planned to live in Wyoming or some other ranching state. Which of course she didn't, but nevertheless...

"They have something called a flight zone that handlers need to respect. In a corral situation the handlers are already deep in the bison's flight zone, so the animals are in a moderate state of fear. All it takes is sudden movement or a loud noise, just about anything can cause the bison to go into a high state of fear, and that's when they start crashing fences or goring other animals, or in this case the handler. Mike was lucky today. It could have been a lot worse."

"And this from the man who wants nothing to do with his father's ranch." Lizzie's deadpan analysis hit the bull's eye. Cole turned his head enough to meet her smart-aleck eyes, planning to deliver an irritated stare, but the instant their eyes met they both broke into laughter. She'd called him out. What else could he do?

Maybe it was a way to de-escalate the tension from the medical emergency they'd just worked on together, or maybe she shot from the hip about ranching and he got the message, but, whatever the reason, they spent the rest of the ride into the clinic making immature comments about the cowhand who'd been gored in the backside by a bison. Childish, yes. Shamelessly enjoyable? Yes again.

Had he ever laughed until his sides hurt with Victoria?

"So a bison handler walks into a bar…" Yeah, she cracked herself up as she proceeded to tell a horrible rendition of a classic joke. He laughed along, but he also got a kick out of how "bar" sounded like *bah* and "handler" like *handlaw* when she said it, and that made him enjoy the joke even more.

Cole never acted this way with his medical peers, even if sometimes he wanted to. Nope, he always kept it professional. But then this was Lizzie, and they'd just discovered they could let their hair down together.

Which set off a whole other fantasy.

To help get his mind off his growing desire for Lizzie, he jumped right into bragging incessantly to Lotte and Rita the instant they got back to the clinic. "You should have seen her…"

Tuesday morning Cole sent out texts to several medical-community friends he knew on the east coast, fishing for information on their internal-medicine resident programs. Then he got right to work at the clinic while he waited for information to roll in. Lizzie stopped by and handed him a list of her second-string hospitals, as she'd promised. She'd definitely made her sights more realistic this time around, but he didn't have a contact at a single one of those hospitals.

Midmorning, while completing a surgery referral for cholelithiasis in a forty-five-year-old woman, he got a call.

"Cole, it's Larry."

Lawrence Rivers didn't call unless there was a good

reason. Wasn't that how Trevor had wound up with Elisabete Silva? "Hi, what's up?"

"What are you doing weekend after next?"

"I'll be right here in Cattleman Bluff until my brother gets back, why?"

"I saw your text about resident spots and I thought I'd save you some time."

"How're you going to do that?"

"One of the internal-medicine first-year residents may be dropping out of our program for an assortment of personal reasons."

"Are you serious?"

"Yeah, but no one knows about it yet, and it's not a sure deal. Here's the thing, weekend after next is the annual JHH charity event, right? They're having a formal affair at Hotel Monaco in Baltimore, and most of the east-coast hospital administrators will be there, including the resident admin from Boston University Hospital. Even if Lizzie can't get in at our program in Boston, she can meet and make a good impression on a boatload of other administrators. It'd be a good time to try out your Professor Henry Higgins and Eliza Doolittle routine, don't you think?"

Cole sat in order to take in everything his friend told him. Was that what he'd become where Lizzie was concerned—even bigger than a cliché, a George Bernard Shaw character?

Pygmalion aside, Cole promised Lawrence that Elisabete was hirable, beyond hirable, then he told him all about the recent goring incident. He owed her a hand up, not only for her, but for Flora's future. He could introduce her to a number of important people there and if she made a good impression at the charity event she was bound to find a resident program sooner rather than later. She had a baby to support, she needed a job when Trevor and Julie got home, which was only a few weeks away.

"Send the invitation. We'll be there."

After Cole hung up a long list of worries queued up in his mind. Would Lizzie even agree to going? Would she be prepared for the upscale event? She certainly didn't have the wardrobe for a charity ball at a grand hotel; he'd have to buy her a dress. And not let on what his intentions were, because she'd have a fit if she knew it was a setup. His outlook grew grim, but he was determined to make this opportunity work for her.

If he was successful she'd meet and impress the perfect hospital administrator who'd find a place for her either in the current resident program, or maybe give her some sort of hospital staff position while she waited for next year's list of openings.

All Cole could do was put her in the right place at the right time. The rest would be completely up to Lizzie to make the magic happen. Which was why he'd have to step up their nightly medical conversations, and, while she wasn't looking, sneak in a few tidbits about proper charity-ball etiquette.

He rubbed his palms together, then quickly got lost in another thought—if he was successful, he might never see her again. Some of the excitement dissipated.

Wednesday, Cole beat Lizzie home from work and found the large package he'd ordered the other morning waiting for him. He tore open the cardboard box to get to the baby jumper seat inside. A bright and friendly-looking, freestanding baby jumper required assembly, so he got right to work in order to surprise Lizzie, and most especially Flora, when they got home.

The rotating, comfortable-looking seat would let Flora's legs dangle and her toes touch the ground, which would help develop large motor skills when she pushed off and jumped. Plus, it would be a safe place to keep her while Lizzie needed both of her hands. Like, for instance—and the true reason he'd gotten it—while they sat at the dinner table. Flora could dangle, jump and play with the colorful creatures and attached toys to her heart's content.

Once he'd finished the setup, Cole smiled, taking great joy in getting something special for Flora. The more time he spent around her, the cuter she got, and sometimes, when the timing didn't work out right and he didn't see her, he missed her.

Had he once missed Victoria's son, Eddie? Nope.

Midgrin, Lizzie breezed into the kitchen with Flora in her car carrier seat, and Cole stood proudly beside the jumper toy waiting for them to reach the dining room. Flora was making some loud baby sounds, not fussing, just exploring her voice, and once Lizzie pushed through the door she stopped on a dime.

"What's this?"

"Flora's new jumping toy."

"You got this?" He nodded. "Did you know that Gina has one of these at her house and she says Flora loves it?" He shook his head. "Oh, my Gawd, Flora, lookie!" It might as well have been Christmas.

Lizzie set the car carrier on the dining table and Cole did the honors of taking Flora out, enjoying the sturdy feel of her growing body. "Look at this, Flora. What do you think?" Her little legs started kicking before he could even set her in the seat. She squealed the minute her bottom hit the vinyl. Cole flipped on the switch and loud jungle-animal sounds started along with silly music. The baby loved it and kicked her legs, setting off more bouncing.

A tight squeeze on his arm drew his attention away from Flora to Lizzie. She looked sincerely up at him. "This is so sweet of you. Thank you."

"My pleasure." And it was, since he enjoyed watching Flora almost as much as Lizzie.

The love he saw in Lizzie's eyes for her daughter seemed to reach inside his chest and grab his heart. What must that kind of love feel like? One thing he knew for sure, the simple gift had brought a roomful of joy into the house, and he wouldn't trade having the two of them here for anything.

And yet, his most important task at this point in time was to find Lizzie a job and send her away. His wide grin suddenly felt all wrong.

That night after dinner and after Flora had been nursed and put to bed, Lizzie headed to meet Cole in the library loft above the living room. She loved these meetings with him, not only for the wealth of medical knowledge he shared, but also for the one-on-one time alone with Cole. Since he'd kissed her cowboy-style on the open range under that never-ending Wyoming sky, though, he'd pulled back. Way back. Most days he seemed more like the guy she'd originally met when she'd first arrived. Distant and standoffish. Except they'd shared a good belly laugh the other day on the drive back from the Waltons'. And this afternoon he'd surprised the heck out of her with that impulsive gift for Flora. She shook her head, missing the man who'd helped with Flora and who'd diplomatically shown her the error of her pigheaded ways with the clinic personnel when she'd first arrived in Cattleman Bluff. She'd caught a glimpse of who he could be today and wanted more. But all the years in foster care had trained her never to get her hopes up. People never wanted her for long, so they just kept passing her around.

Lizzie didn't have enough time to sort out her confused thoughts. Once she hit the top of the spiral steps to the library, he was already waiting at the table they shared nightly, a hot mug of something steaming to his right. Probably Sweet Dreams herbal tea. A barely there smile didn't come close to his eyes, but he stood and, like a trained gentleman, waited for her dutifully.

"What's on the agenda tonight?" she said, trying to ignore the lackluster greeting, walking heavy-footed toward her chair.

He sat back down and weaved his fingers together, resting his hands on the table between them. "I was wondering if you'd consider taking a trip with me to Baltimore?"

He'd blindsided her with a crazy question and she nearly fell off her chair before she'd completely sat down. "What's in Baltimore?" Was this a test?

"What will be in Baltimore? Nearly every single university-hospital resident-program administrator this side of the Mississippi."

She didn't bother to scoot back into the chair, but stayed balancing on the front edge. "I'm listening."

"Weekend after next the prestigious Johns Hopkins Hospital is hosting their annual charity event, and we've been invited."

"That's where you work, right?"

He nodded.

"Why invite me?"

"Were you not listening? You'll be introduced to the people who can get you into their resident programs. Make the right impression, it can open doors for you."

Nerves twined together making an uncomfortable ball in her stomach. She didn't dare get her hopes up since she'd learned the hard way by failing to get placed this year. Plus she wasn't exactly known for her charm. "I can't do that. I'll blow it for sure."

For the first time since that afternoon with Flora jumping in her chair, she saw an honest reaction from him. He torqued his face in disbelief. "That's not the Lizzie I know. When you put your mind to it, you can do anything."

Did he know her that well?

Feeling like a little girl, she held her breath and glanced upward, her heart jumping its beat. Uncensored honesty kicked in and she let him see the unconfident shadow that followed her everywhere, the part of her she'd locked away all her life in order to get through the tough stuff. Her usual fake facade of confidence and tough Boston girl had been her survival, but right now... He'd pushed her just past her comfort zone, enough to see her true reaction, and she couldn't let him see any more.

Was a measly old charity ball really going to be her undoing?

He must have read her panic and appeared at her side while barely seeming to move. His large hand squeezed her shoulder. "What's up?"

"I don't know how to act around rich people. I won't belong there. I'll stand out like a copper penny with a bunch of silver dollars."

Cole squeezed her shoulder tighter and dropped to her eye level. "Honey, you're the silver dollar. We just need to let them discover that."

Well, that did it. First he bought her baby a wonderful gift, now he paid her the sweetest compliment she'd ever heard. She flung her arms around his neck and hugged him tight to hide the unwelcomed tears springing up and dripping over her lids. His arms wrapped around her back, one warm hand massaging up and down. She thought she could stay like this for eternity and never get tired of Cole holding her—and how she'd missed him since their kiss—but she needed to pull herself together. There were at least a hundred questions she had right that instant, and she figured she'd think of a thousand more as the night went on. He'd just proved he had confidence in her; the least she could do was not let him down. "How do we pull this off? And, yes, I did say 'we' because there's no way I can do this without you."

He pulled back and passed her the sincerest and handsomest gaze she'd ever seen. It made her instantly want to drop to her knee and ask him to marry her. God, she was easy. And starved for love!

"I'll be by your side every step of the way." He kissed her forehead—more like a friend than a man she had the hots for, but right now was no time to protest—broke away from their hug and sat over by his steaming mug of herbal tea again. Back to business. "I'll teach you everything you need to know to knock the argyle socks off those nerdy admins. We'll buy you a dress they won't be able to take their eyes off of, and basically all you'll have to do is smile."

She wiped at the dregs of her tears. "That sounds a little smarmy. And really sexist."

"I'm just saying." His brows pushed down, clueing her in he was only trying to be helpful and had exaggerated maybe "a ttch"—wasn't that the word he liked to use? But his dark eyes let out that little twinkle she sometimes saw when she amused him. "You do have a beautiful smile, you know."

He thought she had a beautiful smile? Her head spun at the news. She blurted the first coherent words that came to mind. "I can't let you buy me a dress."

"You're sure as hell not wearing those unisex slacks and button-up blouses of yours."

"Good point." She shook her head again; there really was no way she could go to this event without his help because she needed every penny she made at the clinic. "I'll pay you back."

"Whatever. Here's the thing—we need to go shopping in town this weekend. Rita told me about a flashy new boutique that's recently opened, and it just so happens I treated the owner for a gallbladder attack today and she gave me a discount card. Small world, eh?"

So that was what he was shooting the breeze with the clinic receptionist over today. Lizzie had to admit it had burned a little to see him spread that Wyoming gentleman charm around, especially with the sexy blonde. Her sensibilities wouldn't let up. "I'm already feeling like a kept woman. Your brother gave me a job, a place to live, and now you're buying me clothes."

"Don't look at it that way—be practical. We hired you with room and board as part of the package. Look, this is necessary in order to make the best impression. You'll thank me for it one day."

"Only after I pay you back." Wait, wait, wait! "No. See. I can't go. What about Flora? Who'll take care of her while I'm at this party?"

"First off, it's not a party, it's a fund-raising event." He licked his lips before following up on his next thought. "I was thinking we'd leave Saturday morning and return Sunday morning. One night. I'm pretty sure Gretchen could take care of Flora for one night."

"Leave my baby? Are you trying to kill me? I'd be so miserable without her, there'd be no way I could be the silver dollar you insist I can be."

Silvah dawla.

"*Are.* You are. Get it?" He leveled his gaze and stared hard at her, and he wasn't going to let up until she agreed. "You'll be you on your best behavior."

"I won't be able to concentrate on anything but Flora. I'll be crying the whole time, ruining the new dress. How can I be charming without my baby?"

"How do you get through work every day?"

"By knowing I get to come home and see her."

"And you will see her. It's just twenty-four hours I'm asking for."

She'd been storing up extra breast milk for the sitter, and Gretchen had proved to be amazing with her baby—would it really be impossible to leave Flora for one day? Especially since this event in Baltimore could change their future for the better? It wouldn't be wise to miss this opportunity. She had to think for two now.

She curled in her lower lip, trying her best to be a team player. And since when had they become a team? "Why go to all this trouble for me?"

"Because I want the best for you, Lizzie. This one night can open doors for you and your daughter's future. Sacrifice one night for your entire future."

He'd punched a heart-shaped hole in her chest with those words. The man was for real. She'd taken a last-ditch job in Wyoming out of desperation, but it turned out she'd come to the best place she'd ever been and face-to-face with the noblest man she'd ever met. She cleared her throat. "Well, what if we don't find a dress in town?"

He laughed at her weakest line of protest yet. "Then we'll go online and use overnight shipping."

She wanted to hate him for being persistent, but loved him for putting up with her. For not giving up. No man had ever done that before, and that tiny swell of love cut loose. It must have shown in her eyes. "You think you have all the answers, don't you?"

His tolerant gaze shifted to the look she remembered after they'd made out by the horses. "In this instance, I know I do." That sizzling dark stare set off a reaction distinctly below her waist.

She was a fool for confident men; the fact her breasts tightened and peaked beneath her T-shirt proved it. She and Cole were having one of those moments that seemed to happen more frequently before that first kiss—the kind where sparks flew both ways—and without saying a word each let the other know something amazing could happen if they let it. But with this new turn of events, most specifically the charity ball, Lizzie needed to keep her head about her. She couldn't let herself get swept away in the big cowboy's supersexy eyes. She hated to do it, but if he wanted to train her up and send her away, she'd have to break this spell because they had plans to make, and work to do.

"I believe you," she whispered, sitting back in her chair, letting their moment trickle away. "So let's get started."

A cloud of disappointment scudded across his gaze but he synced in with her, sat and acted as if nothing short of a hot and sweaty promise had just passed between them. He took a drink from his mug and opened the four-inch-thick Johns Hopkins *Internal Medicine Board Review* book; next to that was an equally thick *Pathologic Basis of Disease* tome. "Okay, then."

Back to business as usual.

Saturday Cole insisted they duck out from the ranch around lunchtime for the boutique on Main Street and Lizzie arranged for Gretchen to watch Flora. They'd timed it to work around her nap. He'd quizzed her over her size and what her best colors were all morning, and had called ahead so some dresses were pulled and ready to try on. Evidently he had limited time because he was bringing his father's bookkeeping up to date, a major job he'd moaned about on the drive over. Of course she loved his sharing his concerns with her, so she kept her mouth shut and let him vent.

Lizzie'd had minimal time on her own since arriving in Cattleman Bluff and, though she'd been meaning to check out the shops, she'd yet to make it into this part of town. She gazed in amazement as they walked under an arch made entirely from elk antlers stretched across a street that could double as an old Western movie set, raised timber boardwalks and all.

"It's the largest in the state," Cole said nonchalantly, knowing exactly what she reacted to. "Jackson Hole has a pretty good one, but nothing like this." He glanced upwards, and she studied the arch closer up.

Was this something to be proud of? "Interesting," was all she could think to say.

The boutique was tiny with only two dresses on display in the window, and both looked far too Western and lacy for a girl from Boston, but she'd keep an open mind since Cole had gone to such an effort.

The owner, Carol, waited excitedly inside. "Hi! Come in. Those are the dresses I thought you might like." She pointed to a rack with four dresses hanging on it right next to a fitting room.

Expecting to see gowns more suited for matronly types, Lizzie was surprised to find a colorful assortment of flirty full-length gowns. She checked the size and worried that since the baby she wouldn't be able to pull off looking sexy. She could always use control underwear for her leftover baby bump, though.

Without looking at Cole, because she was suddenly hit with a pang of embarrassment having to model gowns for essentially her boss, the sexy guy she had a crush on, she grabbed the black one and another red dress and scooted inside the tiny cubicle. She slipped out of her clothes as quickly as possible and first tried on the black one.

"No way!" she said from inside the fitting room. "This one is cut to my waist. I'm not wearing it."

"Okay. I won't argue, but feel free to show me if you want." She heard the teasing, and maybe a twinge of hopefulness in his playful response. Turning sideways, realizing her post-baby figure was definitely curvier, she toyed with the idea of modeling for him. *Yeah. No.* Her new-mother breasts poured out, giving her a cleavage she'd never had before. *He's not seeing me in this.* Then she wiggled out of it and moved to the red one.

"What's this red one called?"

"That's a mermaid dress. You like it?"

The red velvet and lace dress looked more suited for winter than a summer event, but she did like the neckline and the capped sleeves. "I like the cut on it, but I'd like something a little more summery."

"Oh, then, try this one on."

It must have been hanging on the rack, too, because Carol pushed a few hangers across the bar and managed to find something in record time. She handed it over the top of the fitting-room door before Lizzie could get out of the red one.

In pale icy blue, the beaded bodice was offset by laced cap sleeves with sequined stripes and had a sweeping, gauzy skirt flared by wispy godets. A triangle cutout on the back made for fun peekaboo sexy appeal without showing too much skin. She liked it. Really liked it, and hoped it looked as good on as it did on the hanger.

It had lined and lightly padded cups in the front, so she wouldn't need a bra, but her breasts spilled over the classic cut. The fitting bodice actually did all the girding she needed in her waist, and the flow of the skirt made her feel feminine and even a little playful. The question was, what would Cole think of it?

She zipped as far as she could, then needed Carol's help with the hook-and-eye parts.

The woman gasped when she came into the compact room. "You look gorgeous. Oh, honey, this is definitely your color." Carol filled Lizzie to the brim with compliments as she hooked the dress. Then she stepped back, honest to goodness envy in her eyes. "This one's made for you."

Lizzie liked the dress, for sure, but was it really perfect for her? How could she know? She'd never worn an evening gown in her life. Dared she show Cole? He'd see her soon enough, but, hey, the man was paying for this dress, so he deserved to put in his two cents, right? Maybe he'd hate it.

She inhaled and stepped out of the fitting room, and the first chance she got to catch Cole's reaction she glanced at his face. The best she could describe his expression was astonished. Astonished? Really, he was that stunned by her putting on a fancy dress?

She'd let her hair out of the confining rubber band and it hung loose around her cap sleeve–covered shoulders, and she stood on her toes, since the dress required heels she didn't have, which made her feel a little off balance. Or maybe it was Cole's continuing awestruck stare.

"This dress was made for Lizzie, don't you think?" Carol said, gesturing with both hands toward her.

Cole was evidently dumbstruck, only nodding his agreement. Had she ever affected a man like this in her life? As though he were seeing her for the first time, an array of expressions crossed his face in the span of one moment. Amazement, surprise, reverence, desire. Yes, he'd been unable to hide that part, desire, and seeing his reaction made Lizzie feel beautiful from the tip of her head all the way down to her unpainted toenails. A cascade of chills covered her skin; she needed to look away, and so she spun around and pretended to be distracted by the dress, not his reaction to it.

"Is this the one?" she asked over her shoulder, insisting on sounding blasé.

"Definitely," he said, and when she chanced one last

glance at him his stare seemed to say, *You're the one.* It shocked and frightened her, making her breath quiver, and she headed for the fitting room hoping he didn't notice.

Maybe she'd imagined his reaction. Or hoped for it. No. She couldn't get her hopes up about Cole Montgomery. The thought of them as a couple was absurd, and...

"Okay, boss. Thanks. I like it too." She did everything in her power to play down the depth of emotions rolling through her. For that one instant, all she wanted in the world was to be *the one* for him. And wasn't that the biggest fool's dream she'd ever invented? Because in her world people always let her down and she couldn't trust them. Especially men.

A little voice in her head countered that Cole had kept his word about everything since she'd met him, even about not kissing her again.

"You'll need shoes." Carol broke into her thoughts.

"Oh, right. My flip-flops won't exactly do this justice, even though they have rhinestones." Self-deprecating humor seemed the only route to take right now, because otherwise she'd have to admit that something substantial had happened between them. She wasn't anywhere near ready to deal with that. Or the significance.

"Try these on." Carol was the fastest shop attendant she'd ever encountered. Usually she'd have to hunt them out in the stores where she shopped, then beg for assistance.

Four-inch strappy silver heels got slid under the changing-room door, ensuring Lizzie would have to get a pedicure to go to this event. And what about her hair? Oh, my, her head was spinning with how disruptive this plan of Cole's had become.

"Get whatever you need," he said.

"What about a necklace?" Carol was quick to add.

"I'll take care of that," Cole said. "Thanks."

His comment started a whole new wave of chills circling Lizzie's body, but the feeling quickly waned. Was
Cole doing this because he cared or because he wanted
to get rid of her?

CHAPTER EIGHT

ALL THE MAGIC and fairy dust disappeared the moment they got back in the car. Cole seemed suspiciously quiet, as if he'd pulled himself together, or had given himself a stern talking-to, and the ride home felt nothing short of awkward. All of Lizzie's quick *what if?* thoughts and fanciful dreams of being his lady dissolved into the thick, odd atmosphere inside the car.

Once safely back at the homestead, all business again, Cole dropped Lizzie off at the front of the house and he took off for the ranch office in the stables. It was as though their moment had never happened, as if what he'd done for her was routine and his desirous gaze had only been in her imagination, and now it was time for him to get on with the show. Bookkeeping called.

"Thanks again!" she said for about the fifteenth time since leaving the boutique as he walked away. Crushed, she stood holding the dress in a travel bag, compliments of the store. So this was how Cinderella felt after the ball.

"You're welcome. You'll knock 'em dead next weekend." He kept walking, didn't even glance back.

She'd never forget that look today when he had seen her in that dress. Never. It had made her shiver from her very center, down her spine and to the tips of her toes. What would it be like? She sighed and walked toward the house.

The thought of going to this huge event and having to be on top form scared her to death, and there was only one person in the world who could calm her down right now. Flora. With a smile, thinking how much progress Flora had made since coming here, Lizzie entered the house. She'd barely got inside when she found Gretchen laughing and singing along with the repetitious songs coming from the new baby jungle Jumperoo, and Flora squealing with joy, bouncing to her little heart's content.

Lizzie owed Cole so much, the least she could do was knock 'em dead next weekend. For him. Then get out of his life as soon as possible. It seemed he'd want it that way.

On Monday all the exam rooms were filled with patients by the time Lizzie got to work. She'd spent a little extra time talking with Gina, whom she'd come to really like, and wound up being a little late. Cole was already seeing his patients, and she was thankful to dive right into work. Lotte handed her the schedule and made a disapproving expression as she filled Lizzie in on her first patient.

"This one's trouble," she said. "Typical spoiled teenager who keeps coming up with reasons to miss school. Last month it was nausea and vomiting. Before that insomnia. Maybe if she spent less time online she'd get enough sleep. Today, she's got a headache. Good luck." She huffed and walked away, and when Lizzie caught a glimpse of Cole leaving one exam room and entering another she rolled her eyes rather than say what was really on her mind.

Having the prediagnosis of faking it drummed into her head by the overbearing nurse, Lizzie did what Cole had suggested in order to keep peace at the clinic and bit back her first thoughts. But she was bound and determined not to step into that room with a preconceived opinion of what was wrong with her fourteen-year-old patient.

When she did enter the examination room, what she

found was a withdrawn and anemic-looking young teen named Valerie with mousy brown hair and intensely sad gray eyes. It was a look that didn't seem easily faked, and, being only twenty-six, Lizzie still prided herself in seeing through teenage drama. Valerie's mother looked as tense as the daughter, and nearly at her wit's end. Both mother and daughter were nail biters, and both were underweight—not that that had anything to do with diagnosing a headache, it was just an observation, and family dynamics often played into teenage headaches. The first thing Lizzie did was dim the light in case Valerie had photophobia.

"I just don't know what it's going to be next," the mother said, not waiting for a proper introduction or trying to hide her exasperation.

"I'm Dr. Silva." Lizzie kept to her usual routine, offering her hand to the patient to shake, and then her mother. "I've read through your history, Valerie, and I see you've had some problems with stomachaches in the past couple of months?"

"That was from taking too many over-the-counter headache pills." The mother insisted on doing all of the talking.

"How long have the headaches been going on?"

Valerie actually opened her mouth to reply, but her mother beat her to it. "A couple of months."

"Any correlation with the menstrual cycle?"

Mom looked to Valerie, who shook her head, and it seemed even that small move aggravated the pain.

"How long do the headaches typically last?"

"A few hours." Valerie's high-pitched, tinny voice sounded younger than she looked. "Sometimes a whole day. Once two days. I woke up with this one today and I think it started last night."

Lizzie understood that migraines presented differently

in adolescents than adults and didn't usually last as long. So far she hadn't ruled out migraine.

"Show me where it hurts." Valerie touched both of her temples. Again, Lizzie understood that migraines in adolescents could be bilateral instead of unilateral as for most adults. "Can you describe the pain?" The teenager gave her a blank look, so she decided to prompt her. "Does it throb or pulsate?"

"Throbs." Valerie sounded on the verge of tears. "Anything I do makes it feel worse."

"Have you vomited today?"

"No, but I can't eat. Just the thought makes me want to barf. Why does this happen to me?"

"I can imagine that these headaches would be frustrating, Valerie. Is it okay if I ask you a few more questions before I examine you?"

The reluctant patient nodded.

After completing a thorough history to establish any symptoms that might precede the headaches like auras, and to help rule out depression and anxiety, since they often coexisted with migraine headaches in adolescents, Lizzie discovered Valerie had pretty classic symptoms. Difficulty thinking, light-headedness, and general fatigue along with the nausea and vomiting and photophobia. Valerie said it even hurt to listen to music when she had the headaches—phonophobia.

With the physical examination Lizzie discovered Valerie also had neck tension and pain, but the rest of the examination, including basic eye exam and neurological testing, proved normal. She still had a hunch her young patient might also be dealing with depression.

Lizzie's biggest job today would be to make sure these were primary headaches, not secondary to another condition such as a tumor, concussion or sinus disease, or several other potentially life-threatening conditions.

"I'm going to recommend something called a CT scan for now, and once we have that information we can move forward with treatment."

"Does she have a brain tumor?" Panic sliced through the mother's voice.

"I don't believe so, but we need to perform standard protocol testing first. I think your daughter has classic early-onset migraine headaches, and we can treat that." She glanced at Valerie, who showed the first sign of hope today. "First we have to make sure what's going on, okay?"

The mother agreed and Lizzie wrote the referral for a stat CT scan at the radiology center the next town over, a forty-minute drive, but well worth it for the concerned mother and daughter. This would buy her time to discuss the medical treatment for adolescent migraine sufferers with Cole tonight in their routine after-dinner meeting.

Now that Lizzie had a car to drop off and pick up Flora from child care at Gina's every day, she arrived home just in time to nurse her baby and change clothes for dinner. When she showed up at the dining table only Gretchen and Monty were there.

"Cole said not to wait, he had an errand to run," Gretchen said as she passed a plate of pasta toward Lizzie. "Oh, but he said he'd expect to see you at eight in the library like always."

Her initial disappointment lessened. "Okay. Thanks." Lizzie put Flora in her bouncing chair, making sure the sound was off out of respect for Monty. She suspected the elephant and monkey sounds got on his nerves after a while. Flora didn't seem to notice and immediately started jumping and playing with the attached plastic spinning ball filled with colorful beads.

She helped Monty dish out a few extra meatballs, while wondering where Cole had gone and what he might be doing. She didn't have the right to any part of him beyond the clinic and what time they shared in his home, but after last Saturday, when he'd bought her the dress with his seal of approval, she'd felt differently about him. Like she might be falling in love. Couldn't help it. As usual she'd overreacted to his consideration. Was she that starved for attention?

Monty was his usual cantankerous self, complaining about the home-health aide the hospital sent out each day. "Why'd they give me a guy? I can handle letting a woman bathe and dress me. Hell, I don't even need the help with Gretchen around, and this guy has hands like bears."

"My condolences to his wife," Lizzie tossed in drily, hoping to knock Monty off balance and maybe get him to change the topic.

"I doubt he has one," he grumbled under his breath before shoving in half a meatball. All complaining aside, she was happy to hear him talk so much. Each day his words and strength got better. Such a positive sign.

"Will you let me bathe Flora tonight?" Gretchen made a concerted effort to change the topic, too. "Now that she's in child care, I miss her so much." She glanced at the baby and made a silly grandmotherly face.

"You don't have to do that." Lizzie missed Flora after her days at work, too.

"I want to. I can get her all ready for you, then you can read her a story and put her to bed. How's that?"

Lizzie had been making a concerted effort to get Flora in a routine now that she was just about four months old. Bath, nursing, reading a book were all part of her night-time routine.

"Since you put it that way, I'll take you up on it, but you have to let me do the dishes." Lizzie gazed kindly at the silver-haired woman who had stepped in as the matriarch of this ranch, and thought how much she'd miss her when the summer and this job at the clinic ended. She inwardly shook her head, scolding herself for getting involved with everyone and everything in Cattleman Bluff. Especially Cole.

He'd insisted his plan to take her to the charity event was to make sure she had a solid future, but deep inside she wondered if it was just to get rid of her. The sooner, the better.

That thought melted away some of her happy feelings for Gretchen and grouchy Monty as she removed the dishes from the table and walked into the kitchen just in time to see Cole come in. Then a whole new wave of mixed-up feelings took over.

"Hi," he said, looking steadily at her, his demeanor calm.

"Hi." Her heart got flighty but she recovered quickly enough. "You need some dinner?"

"I grabbed a bite at the diner in town."

Why did he need to do that? Had he been as shaken by their moments in the dress boutique the other day as she'd been? He'd been nowhere to find on Sunday, and had seemed to only slip in and out of his office like a ghost all day today.

He kept walking. "I'll see you at eight."

She dipped her hands in warm dishwater and stared at the window, hoping to follow his reflection on the glass, but it was summer and still too light out. Instead she turned and watched his broad back as he continued on into the house, those big shoulders she'd come to rely on, then she tried to read the closed-down vibes lingering in his wake.

Fortunately she had a lot to do between now and eight, so she couldn't stand around smelling the lemon dish soap wondering what was up with Cole, even though she doubted she'd be able to get him out of her mind no matter what.

* * *

Eight o'clock, Lizzie came prepared for their meeting with a specific goal in mind—how best to treat her new patient. Plus she brought her own mug of tea tonight.

As always, Cole had beat her there and sat reading a medical journal while waiting, the light bulbs casting a yellow tint, making his skin almost golden. He glanced up and smiled, and she thought how much she loved the grooves along his cheeks whenever he did.

"I caught you being good today," he said.

What part of the day was he referring to? The clinic? The kitchen earlier? "Why does that make me think of grammar school?"

He went thoughtful, his glance downward. "Maybe because my mother used to say that to me."

"When you were ten?" She was touched by the memory of his mother, but didn't have a clue what was going on so she took the smart-aleck route.

"Probably." His smile settled into more of a pensive expression. "But I was talking about your holding your tongue with Lotte at the clinic this morning, and again later in the day when she insisted her way of teaching asthmatics how to use inhalers wasn't out of date."

Now she laughed. "Ah, so you could tell I had to zip my lips both times, but mostly for her being so judgmental about my patient." She put down her mug and stood beside her usual chair.

"Your body language is pretty easy to read." He shifted forward in his chair, put his forearms on the table. "Yes, that's exactly what I'm talking about, and I thought you wanted to deck her." His brows tented and his gaze drifted toward hers. "I especially liked how you explained to her, after the appointment, how sometimes teenagers really are sick. I think she got your point without your blowing up or her feeling reprimanded. Anyway, nice job. Shows me you can learn and change."

Now his smile came back full force and she decided not to keep being a wiseacre. "If you don't mind, I'd really like to discuss Valerie's case with you. Especially the treatment."

"Of course. We can learn together because teenage migraines are definitely out of my wheelhouse."

Instead of sitting across from Cole, as she always did, she put her books next to her mug and pulled the chair next to his. "We can read together," she said, enjoying the scent of his masculine soap. She could sit and stare into his mesmerizing eyes all night, but that wouldn't help her form an assessment and plan for her newest patient. Sitting beside him would actually help her focus…once she got used to how good he smelled. As if that would ever happen.

She opened the textbook on adolescent health and read about the similarities and differences between adult and adolescent migraines.

"I've sent her for a CT scan, which I'll bet my next paycheck will be negative. But I get the feeling she has some emotional issues going on, too. I think she might be depressed, as well. Can we refer to mental-health clinics?"

"You can. Might be a good idea. But it would be up to her mother to get her there and whether or not to pay for the extra psychiatric care. And the best place would be Cheyenne."

"I know some people have a stigma about that, but I want to make sure Valerie knows that teenage depression is more common than she thinks. I don't want her to feel like she's a freak or anything."

"Do you think she might open up one-on-one with you? Maybe you could feel out her situation more that way before you refer her to psych."

"Good point. To her credit, Lotte did fill me in on a few things. Evidently Valerie's mom and dad got divorced last year and there were some nasty accusations being flung around by the Mrs."

"So it was a lousy divorce."

"Aren't they all?"

"Wouldn't know, haven't been married. My parents adored each other."

Is that why you've never married? Afraid you can't duplicate what your parents had?

He opened his laptop and, rather than discuss marriage anymore, they went to several pharmaceutical websites and studied up on medical treatment for teenagers.

"Jeez," Lizzie said. "So many of these migraine drugs aren't approved for adolescents. Our choices are minimal."

"Well, you don't want to go too crazy with meds right off. Looks like treatment should be multimodal with non-pharmacological interventions and modifications in daily living first."

"Agreed. I need to get her on board about noticing triggers and keeping track of what to avoid. That's another reason I'd like some one-on-one teaching time with her."

"If you can address her stressors and any potential mood disorders, that'd be a big help, too."

"We can start her out on nonsteroidal anti-inflammatories and acetaminophen, see how that goes, but the key is to catch the headache early. I'll have to really drive that point home to Valerie and her mother."

"Maybe hold off on triptans for now. See how early treatment works, first?"

"Yeah, that makes sense," she said. "Especially since there's only one or two of those serotonin-binding drugs FDA-approved for teens, plus she'd have to be able to inject it at school if needed and that'd be a whole other learning curve."

"Let's wait for the CT results and go from there. I think you've got your plan mapped out well enough for now."

"Thanks, I feel better discussing it with you."

Once the business-as-usual portion of their meeting was wrapping up, Lizzie recognized tension rolling back into her. If she'd known how life-altering the simple act of trying on a dress could be on their relationship, she'd never have agreed to do it.

Cole kept looking sideways at her as if there was something he wanted to bring up, and suddenly she needed to move her chair back to the other side of the table. How could one man wreak such havoc with her mind?

He reached into his shirt pocket and pulled out a small black velvet pouch cinched together by a ribbon. "I got to thinking about the charity ball and your dress, and, like Carol said, you need a necklace and earrings to go with it, so I went by the town jeweler's after work and found this." He reached for her hand, since her mind was too boggled by his statement to think about physically responding, then he dropped the velvet pouch into her palm. "If you don't like them, take them back and get something else."

"I…I can't accept jewelry from you."

"Well, you can't very well wear that dress without a necklace and earrings either."

"Why'd you do this?"

"How much explaining do you want? Because I haven't got all night. Now open it and try them on." His attempt to imitate Tiberius Montgomery fell far short, but it did get across the fact she needed to check out the gift. Or was it a gift? Might he expect something in return?

Nah, they'd been through that already and he'd proved to be the perfect gentleman. Something else that was aggravatingly appealing about him.

She loosened the black satin ribbon and shook out a huge aquamarine teardrop on a braided silver chain, with matching drop earrings, and forgot how to breathe. "This is gorgeous. It's perfect for that dress. But I can't accept this gift."

"Seriously?"

"This seems so personal and we hardly know each other…um, that way."

"Then let's be practical. I'm dragging you to a function that requires a certain level of sophistication. It's my responsibility to make sure you fit in. Trust me, this necklace won't compare to the jewelry you'll see there, but it will definitely look good on you. I want you to have it and feel confident."

She dared to look into his eyes and realized something serious was whirling around behind those dark lashes. This meant something more than going to an upscale job-placement fair, and she wasn't ready to figure out exactly what that was. Because then she'd have to fully examine all the confusing feelings she'd been carrying around about Dr. Montgomery, and it might set her up to get hurt. "Can I just borrow them for the night?"

He laughed and patiently glanced around the room before answering. "The Cattleman Bluff jewelry store isn't in the business of loaning necklaces. I bought it for you. Keep it. Hawk it. Return it. Your call. But wear it this Saturday night."

"Now I've ticked you off, and I've taken ungraciousness to a new low. Please forgive me, Cole, I'm just not accustomed to a man giving me a dress and a gorgeous necklace. And earrings. Oh, and shoes. No one has ever done that before and it's just, well, I don't know how to describe it." She'd melted down to the babbling stage trying to explain how big a deal this was, and he'd obviously had it with her.

He stood, leaned over the table and took her by the shoulders. The last time a man had been upset with her and had taken her by the shoulders she'd been shaken up pretty good. She tensed. Cole immediately saw the fearful reaction in her eyes and let up, moving one hand from her shoulder to her jaw, gently cupping it. He bent and moved in and, as delicately as a butterfly, kissed her.

"Do me a favor," he whispered next to her ear. She felt the shell of his ear lightly on her cheek. His woodsy after-shave still noticeable on his throat. "Humor me and keep the necklace and earrings. I want to enjoy seeing you in them, and I want to know you might remember me whenever you wear them."

She switched from hard-headed to a puddle of emotion; her hands flew to his cheeks. She kissed him more purposefully than he'd kissed her, and she enjoyed every warm and moist moment. She'd missed his lips. They took their time with the gratitude kiss, but she had no intention of taking it to a different level. Not now anyway. "Thank you. I'll always treasure this necklace and the earrings because you gave them to me."

Wisdom must have kept him from kissing her again, even though she hoped he would. But, perhaps more intimate than any kiss could be, they continued to stare deep into each other's eyes for several more heartbeats. Her gaze flitted around his face, settling on his strong chin and back to those rich brown eyes, searching for some clue for what was happening between them, until it was time to tuck this moment away with all the others and say good-night.

Friday afternoon, Lizzie's last two patients cancelled and she got back to the ranch early. Cole hadn't been so lucky and was still at work. Once again, she was glad for the independence of using Tiberius's car. She'd finished nursing Flora, who'd fallen asleep, and she wandered into the living room.

Monty sat in his chair thumbing through a magazine. The moment she entered he looked up. "Hey, girlie-girl, feel like taking a ride with me?"

"You mean like run an errand?" He'd probably been waiting for her to bring the car home.

"No. Like sit on a horse and saddle. I've missed my horses. Plus the visiting occupational-therapy nurse gave me the okay to ride again today."

"That's great and I'd love to." There was still plenty of light left, being mid-July. "In fact I've wanted to ride again since Cole took me. Let's do it!" Lizzie let Gretchen know what they planned, and, other than looking a little surprised, she switched on the baby monitor on the kitchen windowsill in order to keep tabs on Flora while she slept.

Monty's gait was strong and balanced now, even though he still relied a little on his hand-carved walking stick. The intricately designed wooden cane went well with his dungarees and cowboy hat, too. "I figured you might want to go, already had Jack saddle up Zebulon and O'Reilly for us. We won't do anything strenuous, just enjoy the evening air."

"Sounds great to me, and dibs on Zebulon." Though she expected the ride would conjure up all kinds of heady memories from the afternoon with Cole on the ridge trail.

A half hour later, when she'd been right about her hunch, they'd ridden to a huge corral where the new mothers and calves were kept separated from the grazing steer. Lizzie was proud of the fact she'd remembered everything Cole had taught her about riding, and was handling Zebulon as if she knew what she was doing. For a city girl, she thought she could get used to riding horses.

Monty sat watching the calves nurse for a while, smiling. "I never get tired of my ranch. I especially love the spring when the calves drop, and the summer watching them grow. Makes me know the Circle M will continue on."

Lizzie kept her wondering thoughts, about who would carry on after Monty got too old, to herself.

He made a clicking noise with his mouth and the horses immediately knew it was time to move on. She tightened the inside of her thighs and Zebulon quickened the pace and caught up with Monty and O'Reilly. They continued on, side by side for a while longer, in silence.

"When I was in the hospital in Cheyenne, I was treated like a specimen." Evidently Monty had gotten tired of the quiet. "All these young doctors trotted in every morning and they talked about me and my condition, like I wasn't there."

"I'm sorry."

"That's not my point. I didn't mind that. What I'd forgotten was that the University of Wyoming Hospital is a teaching hospital. They've got a three-year family-medicine program that is supposed to be one of the best in the country. Doctors there learn how to do everything, even surgery, just like Trevor does. That's where he did his residency. I know it's not a fancy job like Cole's but it's just as important. I also know you're a city girl, but I was thinking Wyoming could use more good doctors like you. And that way Flora could grow up in the wide open instead of cooped up in some city apartment surrounded by cement."

No wonder the speech therapist had released him last week; he'd just said more words in one go than he'd said the whole rest of the time she'd been at Circle M. Plus he seemed to read her thoughts about Flora growing up in wide-open spaces.

"Why, Tiberius Montgomery, are you trying to influence my decision?"

"I'm trying to talk some sense into you. Couldn't get through to Cole, but maybe you being a mother and all, well, maybe you'll think about it."

"Cole's gone to great lengths to open some doors for me, but please understand I am honored that you care. And, more importantly, that you think I'm a good doctor."

Maybe she'd gotten too syrupy for Monty or something, but he made that clicking sound again, and both horses picked up speed trotting back toward the ranch and the stables. End of conversation.

Besides thoroughly enjoying the evening ride, regardless of his flighty attitude, Lizzie was flabbergasted that Tiberius Montgomery had given her career any thought. As they dismounted and the stable guy walked off with the horses, an odd niggling, way in the back of her mind, made her promise not to disregard Monty's heartfelt and practical suggestion. Maybe he was on to something.

Walking back to the house she let down her guard and imagined a life with Cole, living in Wyoming, raising Flora together. Her head swirled at the possibility of being his woman. Loving him. Watching him flourish as his fatherly skills grew. Then she stumbled on a rock and nearly fell to her knees. As usual, whenever she got her hopes up about something, the universe had a way of knocking her off balance.

It had been a senseless fantasy anyway. Cole couldn't love her, he was too busy with his career to settle down, and he'd never move home again.

Saturday morning Lizzie was having a fit in her bedroom. "How can I leave my baby?" Those large, pleading eyes nearly broke down Cole's resolve, but there was too much at stake for her to back out now.

Nearly out of patience, Cole paced. If Lizzie couldn't get it through her head that this small sacrifice of twenty-four hours would be worth her entire future, there was nothing more he could do.

He reached for Flora, removing her from Lizzie's

clutches. "Finish packing. I'll take her for a walk." Without giving her a chance to respond, he left with a beaming baby, because Flora always brightened up when Cole held her, and headed for the door. Flora really liked Cole, and Lizzie could tell by his demeanor whenever he held her that the feeling was mutual.

"I'll be back in twenty minutes to get your bags, and we're leaving. Understand?" He gave Lizzie a stern stare, made sure she knew he wasn't horsing around, then, looking at little Flora's happy blue eyes watching his every move, he made a silly face and snorted like a pig as they left. It worked; the baby smiled and squealed, her arms around his neck. "Want to see the horsies?" he asked in a voice a full octave higher than usual. Flora sucked her fist and pumped her feet in answer. "Okay, then. Let's go."

A half-hour later both Lizzie's and his overnight bags were in the trunk of Cole's car and they set off for the airport in Cheyenne, barely speaking a word. He could read her, though, and she was one big ball of fear, separation anxiety and maybe a touch of excitement. He had to admit he was nervous, too. Part of what he was doing felt wrong, as if he'd found and trained a prized mare and turned her into a show horse. Yeah, that definitely didn't feel right, but wasn't it for the greater good? Her greater good?

The thought of not seeing Lizzie every day hit hard. Regardless of whether she got a residency after tonight or not, by summer's end they'd both go their separate ways. He sighed and stepped harder on the gas pedal, nearly hitting eighty on the speedometer.

Lizzie spent the entire drive thinking of things to make calls to Gretchen for, to remind her about caring for Flora. She reached for her phone once again as they parked at the airport, and Cole leaned across the car to stop her. "I think you've covered everything Gretchen needs to know." He forced Lizzie to look at him for the first time that morning. She connected with his eyes, apprehension coloring her expression. "Flora's in good hands. You know it. Now relax and think about rewriting your future tonight."

All she could muster was a nod along with a quivery breath, but at least some of the anxiety fizzled from her gaze.

Forty-five minutes later they boarded their plane and settled in for the three-and-a-half-hour flight. Cole planned to quiz Lizzie part of the time, but as soon as he began she tossed him a glance that begged to be left alone.

Truth was, if she didn't have her routine down by now, cramming for the test would be of little help, so he let her be with her thoughts. Closing his eyes, he faced a fact he wasn't prepared for. What happened after tonight? Or after Trevor and Julie came back to the clinic? Had he done such a great job of shaping up Lizzie that he'd lose her?

The lose part had never been meant to be a part of the equation. This exercise had been a test of his teaching skills. Could he take a young doctor with potential who'd been rejected by all the most prestigious hospitals in the country and turn her into the doctor everyone wanted? His success was supposed to be a feather on his cowboy hat, not an aching, gaping hole in his gut. After spending nearly every day and evening with Lizzie for the past month, he'd grown accustomed to being around her. He looked forward to seeing her serious yet hopeful face each morning and to watching her concentrate each evening in the library as she puckered and smoothed those delicious lips while she read and thought.

What would a day be like without looking into those extraordinary green eyes?

He couldn't go there. Not now. Because right now he needed to work on his act: the guy who was indifferent to her leaving. The guy who only wanted her placed in a resident program so he could get back to business as usual. Busy days in the cardiac clinic at Johns Hopkins, envelope-pushing cardiac procedures, nonstop travel around the country, hell, around the world. Why not? Once she was gone he'd have his old life back.

But since meeting Lizzie, Cole wondered what kind of life that would be.

CHAPTER NINE

LIZZIE HAD AGREED to be ready by 6:00 p.m. and, because her entire future seemed to depend on this blasted event, she didn't want to mess up. Cole had put so much time and effort into making her hirable—even down to scheduling an in-suite mani-pedi at the hotel—she couldn't let him down now.

She'd never been in such a beautiful hotel in her life and she felt like a princess in the huge marble bathtub, the bubbling bath gel smelling of lavender and vanilla, and her toes barely able to reach the end of the tub. She wanted to stay here all afternoon, but knew she couldn't. Wow. Was this how Cole was used to living?

He'd thought nothing of tossing down his credit card to pay for both hotel rooms at the ornate and luxurious Monaco hotel. Until that moment, she hadn't been sure—and sure as hell hadn't been about to ask but had hoped anyway—if they'd be roommates or not.

She'd thought she'd walked into a royal palace when they'd first entered the classic beaux arts building with its sparkling marble floors, crystal chandeliers, grand winding marble staircase and Tiffany stained glass windows. Every bit of history had been preserved yet the lobby was modern and inviting and beyond everything else, due to armloads of flowers in several huge vases, colorful. A girl from Southie, Boston, she'd never had a fantasy come close to the reality of this hotel. Dreams like those were for people who lived in the Back Bay, the upper class of Boston.

Lizzie lay back in the tub and dunked her hair and face under water, suspending herself in time and space. Cole came to mind, as he often did, now. His handsome, all-guy face. His sturdy hands, and how they felt on her shoulders. His lips, soft as a butterfly one moment and demanding the next. The way he heated her up from the inside out with one smoldering glance.

She sat up, the water running down her hair and over her face. The little fantasy from yesterday returned. What would it be like to be his wife, loving him, sleeping with him every night, waking with a smile on her face every day? What if she seduced Cole tonight, to force him to see how good they could be together, to prove she had as much to offer as he did? She'd surprise him with her love, drive him crazy with total passion for him. But she'd know when to leave him alone, too. Yes, they'd be so in touch they'd know without saying what each other wanted. She'd be that kind of wife for him. She dreamed. Plus, they'd be a force to be reckoned with as lovers, and parents. The two of them raising Flora to be... Flora!

Then it hit her: she hadn't thought about Flora in...how long? More proof she was a selfish and terrible mother. She stood up, water falling away, panic replacing the calm she'd just enjoyed. She climbed out of the tub and draped herself in the extra thick and soft bath towel, searching for her cell phone.

Gretchen hadn't called, true, but Cole had probably put the fear of God in her about only calling for an emergency. She speed-dialed and waited.

"Everything's just fine, Elisabete." Gretchen had never called her Lizzie like Monty and Cole. The relaxed sound of the woman's voice poured over Lizzie, automatically helping her calm down. "She's taking her afternoon nap." Baltimore was two hours ahead of Cattleman Bluff; of course it would be nap time for Flora.

"So everything's okay, then?"

"She's as good as gold."

"You're not just saying that, are you?"

"I've never been good at lying, Elisabete. Please trust me with your precious baby. I'm giving her all of my attention. Even Tiberius is helping."

The reassuring words and the sudden sense of family back home put a smile on Lizzie's face. Her little fantasy about Cole returned. She glanced at the crystal clock on the ornate mantle above her hotel-room fireplace. She needed to speed up if she planned to be dressed and made-up by six. And what was she going to do with her hair?

"I'll never be able to repay you. Thank you so much," she said.

"Darlin', you've brought new life back into this family. We love Flora. Now, go and knock 'em dead." Wasn't it interesting how Gretchen naturally considered herself a part of the extended Montgomery family? If Gretchen could, why couldn't Lizzie?

Lizzie hung up, grinning and planning to do just that. But in all honesty, there was only one person she really wanted to knock dead in the figurative sense tonight, and that was Cole Montgomery. She was on to his dirty little plan to get rid of her, but she had a surprise in store for him. Tonight, she'd make him an offer he couldn't possibly refuse…unless ice water ran through his veins. And she'd kissed him enough to know that wasn't the case. Tonight she'd make him want her, no matter what it took.

Decked out in his tux and black dress cowboy boots, Cole knocked on Lizzie's hotel room door at one minute to six, then waited. He'd already made a few calls to various hotel rooms, setting up plans to meet with several residency administrators during the gala cocktails in the Paris foyer. They'd have to wait to see who they'd be sitting with for dinner in the ballroom. Fingers crossed they'd be near the recruiters from Massachusetts General Hospital in Boston and New York Presbyterian Cornell campus since he hadn't been able to contact them so far this afternoon.

The door opened and a vision straight from heaven stood before him. She seemed a little taken aback by seeing him, too. Maybe it was the boots and the Western-styled tux he'd taken out of storage before the trip.

Lizzie's dark hair had been piled in high ringlets on top of her head. Her full brows highlighted those amazing eyes that she'd colored and lined with make-up. Wow. Her skin looked creamy and he fisted his hands inside his pockets to dampen the urge to touch her all over. The ice-blue evening dress fit like a glove, and the choker-style necklace looked perfect on her long neck, the aquamarine stone dangling just below the delicate notch of her throat. If he concentrated, and he definitely was, he could see the faint beating of her pulse there.

She stood watching him taking her all in, waiting with an eager, open gaze. *Well?* He could practically hear her thought.

It required great discipline to speak. "Are you ready?" He couldn't very well let on how overwhelmed and turned on he was by her beauty. Or how his skin practically vibrated with desire. How easily he'd slipped into the most basic of all reactions of a man to a woman. It wasn't the purpose of this night. No, her wow factor was meant for the old tired-eyed doctors recruiting for next year's internal-medicine programs on the East Coast.

But he couldn't ignore the immediate disappointed expression she bore from his silence either and he had to let her know how great she looked. Where had his manners gone? "You look fantastic. I've said it before—that dress was made for you."

She let out her breath. "Whew. Thanks. I don't recognize myself. And by the way, you look sexy as hell."

He stood a little taller, liking that she thought he was sexy looking, and he could think of a million more things to say about how great she looked, too, but this wasn't a date or a mutual-admiration-society meeting. It was business. He couldn't think of tonight in any other way. Tonight was all about the business of getting Lizzie a job. "Got all the names memorized?" Back on track, even though her appearance distracted the hell out of him.

"Yes," she said, turning to pick up her clutch bag, immediately clicking into the purpose of the night. Except he noticed the fine, sequined lace covering the backs of her shoulders and the triangle-shaped cutout area revealing her skin at the center of her back. *What would it be like to touch Lizzie all over?*

She glanced up, a message in her gaze: *touch me, I won't break.* He swallowed and pushed down the desire.

"All you have to do," she said, turning back and straightening to her full height, "is mention the hospital program they're from and I'll remember the name." She glanced at him, narrowed her eyes and nodded. "I'm ready for this, but wish me luck anyway."

She sounded breathy and he lost his train of thought for a moment, thinking of how that breathiness might feel blowing gently across his chest, then on reflex he cupped her upper arm and kissed her cheek. "You're beautiful." He'd meant to wish her luck, but it'd come out wrong.

There was a question in her eyes when he pulled back and he mentally scrambled to cover as he canted his head. "Good luck."

She tucked her lips inward and nodded, seeming suddenly nervous, or disappointed. "I had something else in mind."

"For?" Her dazzling appearance had made him suddenly stupid.

"For wishing me luck." She moved toward him, wrapped her arms around his neck and kissed him hard, her lips already parted.

He sank right into the kiss, could have chucked the whole night for the chance to stay here and seduce her. But that wasn't the kind of man he wanted to be for her. He wanted to help restore her faith in men, not add more evidence to her case against them. He broke off the kiss, but not before her smoldering gaze begged him to take her.

He knew in that moment he wanted her more than any other woman on the planet.

Just not right this instant. They had work to do, a battle to win, a job to conquer. They needed a victory before they celebrated.

He took his pocket kerchief and wiped away the lipstick he instinctively knew she'd left behind on his mouth. Doing his best to recover his breathing and tame the sex-starved beast she'd nearly unleashed with her kiss, he glanced in the mirror in the hotel sitting room, inhaled slowly and let it out.

"You're going to do great," he said, knowing she'd knock dead every doctor she met with her great looks, then impress them with her intelligence and hopefully she'd throw in a little charm. She had it all, he knew beyond a doubt. He had to keep his head clear, for tonight was her night. All she had to do was showcase the polished version of herself.

"Thank you," she said, standing beside him, gazing into the mirror, reapplying lipstick and fixing a few stray curls in her hair, trying her best not to sound disappointed by his not throwing her on the bed and making love to her.

Or was that his thought and disappointment?

He had to focus on the task at hand. Tonight Elisabete Silva was bound to land a job.

"Ready?" He offered his arm.

"As ready as I'll ever be," she said, taking it.

On the elevator ride down to the Paris ballroom he savored the fresh, modern and flirty scent of her perfume, and the way her deep red fingernails matched her toenails. Every part of her had been perfectly put together—even the wisps of hair from the updo falling on her neck seemed flawlessly placed. He was thankful she hadn't lacquered down her hair with spray. He thought all of this while staring straight ahead, watching her reflection in the polished brass elevator door, hoping she didn't notice.

The elevator dinged and the doors parted. A wave of loud chatter hit them as they exited. He glanced at her reassuringly. "Showtime," he said with a confident smile and nod as they stepped onto loud patterned gold-and-maroon carpet and into the ballroom foyer with violet blue walls and ceiling-to-floor magenta velvet curtains.

Cocktails were served in the foyer and they'd taken exactly three steps before a black-vested waiter offered drinks. Lizzie looked to Cole, thinking briefly before accepting a glass of some kind of fun-looking pale cranberry-colored drink.

"What's this?" she asked.

"That's a cosmopolitan, ma'am," the server said, clearly enamored by her beauty. "Vodka, triple sec, cranberry juice and lime."

"Thanks." She took the drink and moved her head close to Cole so no one else would hear. "I'm not nursing tonight and don't plan to keep whatever I express, so why not, right?"

He grinned over the insider information. "Why not?" He took a glass of red wine, and soon his eyes scanned the gathered group for familiar faces. "Ah, George Eckhart, from the Philadelphia program. Follow me." Why waste time?

On task, she took a quick sip of her cocktail and matched him step for step around one group of people then another to reach his mark.

"George! Good to see you."

Dr. Eckhart's eyes reflected respect when he greeted Cole, then they lit up with new interest when Cole introduced him to Elisabete Silva, MD. After that, as hoped and planned for, every doctor he introduced her to reacted nearly identically, and Lizzie became a force to be reckoned with over cocktails.

By 7:00 p.m. someone used a mallet on a brass gong to announce that dinner was served and to direct people to the Paris ballroom. The epic room was set with round dining tables covered in silver cloth, sparkling crystal goblets and the best hotel china and silver, and with vases of white hydrangeas at the center. Cole had checked the seating chart and was happy to see the head of the MGH resident program in Boston would be at their table.

Taking Lizzie's hand, and thoroughly enjoying the feel of her cool fingers wrapping around his, he led her to table number thirty, midway into the ballroom. Dr. Linda Poles might not respond to Lizzie's beauty, but she was sure to appreciate her intelligence and Boston wit. Cole traded a name plate to make sure Lizzie was next to the doctor and watched as the friendly-faced, middle-aged woman in a standard black evening dress approached.

He'd been right, Lizzie and Linda hit it off immediately,

talking about their favorite city, Boston, and the rest of the night played out like a well-rehearsed dream.

By 10:00 p.m. the event was winding down, having raised more money for their cause than on any previous year.

Cole made sure Lizzie bid good-night to Dr. Poles, and also to the doctor from the New York internal-medicine program, Joseph Steinberg, who'd been sitting at a nearby table, and whom Cole had made sure Lizzie had spent time chatting with between the main course and dessert with coffee. Both doctors seemed genuinely taken with Lizzie, as had all the other doctors he'd handpicked to introduce her to tonight. She couldn't have made a better impression.

"Ready to go?" he asked.

"I'd like to finish my drink first." She'd found a favorite in the cosmopolitan and this was her second...or third? But he couldn't fault her since he'd put on so much pressure about tonight. Cosmos or not, she'd performed perfectly.

He took the opportunity to say good-night to a couple more people, glad-handing as he'd never done before, on Lizzie's behalf. After tonight she was bound to get placed in any number of internal-medicine resident programs. She probably wouldn't even have to wait until next year—that was if she was willing to step in late. He stood chatting, hands in pockets, with the wife of another doctor, biding his time until Lizzie was ready to leave, when an arm snaked around his elbow and tugged him near.

Lizzie. "I'm ready." She smiled, that beautiful beam he'd admired all evening, looking no less for the wear over the past few hours.

They squeezed into an elevator with a dozen other people and disappeared into the corner letting everyone else talk and laugh.

"I'll see you to your floor," he made a point to say, since

he had in fact gotten their rooms on different floors so as not to encourage rumors.

"Thanks," she said, fiddling with one of her earrings.

On the fifth floor they both got off, she stepping out of the elevator first. She didn't wait for him, but kept up a quick strut all the way down the hallway. For the first time that night he noticed she maybe wasn't enjoying herself as much as he'd imagined.

"You okay?" he asked before she reached her door.

"As a matter of fact, no."

"Something I do?" This came out of nowhere.

He got the long drawn-out stare, communicating he'd probably just asked the dumbest question of the night, and when she'd made sure she'd gotten her point across she answered. "I'm on to you, Dr. Montgomery." Then she shoved her key card into the slot and pushed her door open.

He stopped right where he was, trying to figure out what was going on. A couple he'd seen at the gala came down the hall, acknowledging him with nods before heading on to their room, but not before he noticed the woman's raised brows. He didn't want to give the wrong impression about him and Lizzie, so he stayed where he was. Just before Lizzie's hotel door banged closed, she caught it with her foot in those strappy silver heels. "You coming in?"

He couldn't very well leave it at that, with her angry, not after all the hoop jumping he'd made her do tonight, so he followed her inside.

Lizzie had felt like a prized pet all night the way Cole had showed her off. She'd gone along with it only because he'd pounded it into her head that this was all about her future. But it didn't feel right.

"What do you mean you're on to me?" Cole asked, from her hotel doorway, one brow raised, an amused glint in his eye.

"You wanted to look good." She folded her arms. "I made you look good tonight."

He narrowed that gaze, tenting his brows, and walked into her sitting room. "What are you talking about?"

"You've made me your pet project, and tonight was the science fair." She made a huge circle with her arms. "I took first prize. You get the blue ribbon."

"Look, Lizzie, that wasn't the case at all. Tonight was all about your making a memorable first impression on the people who will take hundreds of faceless applications and decide who gets into their prized programs and who doesn't. It's a scientific fact that it's harder to reject a person with a face and a personality than a piece of paper with a passport-sized photo on it."

"That's not my point. I felt fake. Like I had to be someone I'm not."

He shook his head and stepped closer to where she'd dug in her heels. "You are Elisabete Silva, in a prettier-than-usual dress, that's all. Oh, and with a great hairdo, too. Meant to tell you that earlier. Not that I don't like the braid and unisex clothes the rest of the time." He worked at a charming smile, but somehow knew how fragile she felt and toned it down.

He looked sincere in wanting to make her feel better, though, and that was what mattered. But she needed to get the next part off her chest. "It's all because you want to get rid of me. Don't lie."

His enticing expression changed to far more serious. "We both knew our time together was temporary. I don't belong at the ranch and you certainly don't belong in that clinic in Cattleman Bluff."

"Who says you don't belong? It's your home."

"Not really. Not anymore." His answer bothered her; didn't he see everything he had in Wyoming? But right now, she needed to stay on point.

"Well, I like it there. I feel connected with the people at the clinic."

"And that's a gift you'll be able to carry with you into your residency wherever you go. When Trevor and Julie come back, they'll take over again. We were only there for the summer. After tonight, your fall and New Year should be set. No, *will be set.* You'll have your choice of programs to accept." He took another step toward her. Why did she feel fragile and invaded, the complete opposite of how she'd felt before they'd left earlier? "We accomplished something special tonight, Lizzie." The tone of his voice modulated to kinder. Gentler. "Flora will thank you one day."

"What about us?" She refused to feel fragile, hated it, made up for it by being brazen. Her fantasy, no matter how silly, deserved a shot. Then she moved closer so she could get a better look at his eyes, since he'd suddenly become evasive with eye contact.

As she expected, he looked perplexed, as if she'd blind-sided him. "A few kisses and a lot of desire doesn't add up to much, does it?"

His words stung, but she warded them off with resolve. She put her hand on his arm, needing to make contact with him. Needing to force him to feel something for her, even if it was only sex. "It could have added up to a lot more, but I get the feeling I'm not good enough for you."

"That's crazy." He nailed her with his disagreeing stare.

"No, it isn't. Your whole goal was to change me. To make me hirable. I mean, I know I came from a completely different background than you. Maybe I seem tough and maybe too aggressive but that's how I survived. I needed to be that way to get by. You've kept me at a distance from the beginning. Like I make you uncomfortable or something. Except for when you needed to teach me stuff. Then I became a project."

"I couldn't take advantage of you. Not that I didn't want you. It wouldn't be right."

"Do you think I'd let you take advantage of me? Come on, whatever you're referring to is mutual. Tonight, though, I think you took advantage of my looking great in this dress." She gave a wry laugh.

"Not so. We seized the moment for you and Flora. You needed tonight. Not me."

"So you could be done with me. Right?" She waited for him to look back into her eyes. "Well, your job is over. Now what?"

He went silent for a beat, cleared his throat. "Now we go back home and finish minding the clinic for another couple of weeks. Then I go back to Baltimore and you'll hopefully have a spot waiting for you in a resident program."

She sighed over his being obtuse, guessing she'd have to spell it out for him. "What about earlier? What about right now?" Her fingers walked up his arm and across his shoulder. "In this hotel room?" She lightly tugged his earlobe.

"That wouldn't be wise."

"Are you always this shut off?"

"I'm your boss. You've had a couple of drinks and you're not using good judgment right now."

"And if I came on to you, you'd be taking advantage of me?"

"Something like that."

"Baloney. I know what I'm doing. I look hot in this dress. Tell me you don't think so." She'd made him look more uncomfortable than she'd ever seen him—and she'd put him in his share of tough positions since she'd moved in to his home and worked with him at the clinic. Her heart pounded with worries he'd shut her down and leave, but she pressed on, needing proof he did or didn't want her as much as she wanted him. "We're in a hotel room and no one will know but us."

"You're playing with fire here. One of us has to be levelheaded—"

"Why?" She'd taken her stand and nothing would turn her back now. She unbuttoned his jacket and slipped her hands inside, exploring his shirt-covered chest and broad back, loving his lingering classic cologne, letting his gorgeous build and rugged face rule her thinking. "I like the fire I see in your eyes." She reached for his jaw, his nostrils gently flared as some of his resistance eased. He did have feelings for her, just as she did for him, and now was the time to let them all out. "I've missed kissing you." Being in heels, she didn't have to lift her chin much to make contact with his lips.

Melding their mouths, tilting her head for better access, she welcomed him full on. His hands shot to her and pulled her tight and close as his tongue delved deep. She moaned with approval. They fought through their kisses without a hint of tenderness. His was a battle of resistance, and hers a fight for what she wanted. Needed. Him. Right now!

Off came his jacket and shirt, and her dress was nearly torn away when he reached the stubborn hook and eye, but he fought them and won. They wound up rolling onto the sitting-room couch, desperate to be naked and making love together. She didn't want him to be gentle, and he couldn't be if he tried. They'd suppressed too much for too long and now was their moment to set everything free.

His hand cupped and pushed up her breast as he kissed her neck and shoulder raggedly. He got rid of his boxers, and she took the moment to look at his imposing figure. Long-waisted, broad shoulders, built for hard work, yet with muscles subdued by his medical career. His strong legs and fully aroused state were a sight she never wanted to forget, but right this moment she needed to touch him.

He moaned when she did, and she eased him back onto the couch as she straddled him, her fingers stroking the smooth skin of his long ridge. His large palms cupped her bottom, massaging the hunger for him, and she dipped her head to his face. They kissed more out of desperation than desire. They'd quickly reached the point where they needed to connect, for him to be inside her, for them to be close and tight and rocking their way to release.

"I'm still nursing and haven't gotten my period yet—" she had to be practical for this one second "—but it's your call. Now's the time."

"I need my wallet," he said, on the exact same wavelength.

Ah, so the traveling cardiologist knew about being prepared. It surprised her, even made her a little jealous, but she took that energy and helped him find and place the condom in record time, rather than let it hold her back.

She stayed on top and controlled his entering her. Things were definitely different since giving birth, but he felt great and she hoped he enjoyed it as much as she did. Glancing at his tense yet euphoric expression, she immediately quit worrying about how she might feel to him. He loved it. She drove him crazy.

He watched her body as she moved on him, worshiping her with his gaze. His hands gripped and guided her hips just so, his head lifting, mouth nipping at her breasts. Now and then his lids dipped closed with pleasure, but he didn't stop looking at her otherwise. She fed his lust, and she loved how that made her feel. Powerful. Wanted. Soon, he needed to go deeper and, with her legs wrapped around his waist and her arms around his neck, he lifted and repositioned her beneath him on the cushions.

He thrust into her fast and frantic and she lost her grasp

on sustaining the pleasure, zipping right along to nearly there and, oops, over the edge. Wow. He groaned all the while her waves of orgasm shot through her spine and down to her toes, and she could feel how her reactions made him harder, brought him closer to release. Soon, with a few long, slow thrusts, he moaned when the moment hit and he hardened even more just before throbbing deep inside.

The whirlwind minutes of having sex with him were worth every risk as her body took over and, having already been shown the way, she came again with a vengeance around him, lengthening his free fall. They rocked together long afterwards, liking the feel of being joined, not wanting it to end. She loved having her breasts crammed against his chest, and the vision from this angle of his straining shoulder muscles while maneuvering the narrow couch. Damn, he felt fantastic and she wished their being together could be more than just now. But knowing Cole as she did, that would never be the case. She'd forced this. He never would have initiated it, being too much of a gentleman. Like always, she'd plowed ahead in her bullheaded fashion and insisted on having her way. With him.

He might be wiser than her, but she glanced up at his face and, from his *What just hit me?* expression, she was convinced he was just as glad she'd forced this completely physical conversation. In fact, it had been long overdue.

After Cole and Lizzie moved to the bed, pulled back the covers and got comfortable snuggling together, he couldn't deny the energy and heat this woman brought him. And when in the last ten years had he performed like that? The thought helped him pinpoint what had been missing with his long string of girlfriends ending with Victoria last year—passion.

From the very first day, Lizzie had managed to pull

out of him the strongest reactions, no matter what the circumstances, be it annoyance, anger, joy, surprise…lust. Oh, yes—lust. And now, realizing there was no place for this relationship to go since she'd be leaving, sadness. He pulled her closer and kissed her forehead; she sighed contentedly, completely relaxed in his arms. All natural beauty, not polished and practiced, just her, the way he liked her. Loved her? The fire that had burned in his belly for her minutes before got replaced with a dull ache of loss.

He inhaled the flowery scent of Lizzie's hair, which had fallen over her shoulders when they'd made love—if he could call it that. What they'd just done had nothing to do with love. It had been totally raw. Focused. Feral. Amazing.

His throat went dry as he prepared to say the toughest thing on his mind, because he knew it was the best thing for her. He pushed aside his selfish desires, for her future. "This can't happen again."

Her head shot up. She stared at him. "Why not? I'm in Wyoming for a few more weeks."

"It's unethical. You're my colleague, not a playmate."

Her brows crinkled in a quizzical way. "And if I like being your playmate?"

"That's beside the point. I'm always on the road. We'll be living in different states. The most we could ask for was the occasional hookup. Is that what you really want?"

"Isn't that how you usually do it? Keep a safe distance from people. Stay too busy to commit to anything or anyone outside of work?"

His hand clutched her shoulder tighter. How had she nailed him so easily? He kept that distance because he'd disappointed everyone who'd ever cared for him, including his mother. He'd never been able to be what those close to him wanted, to be there when they needed him most, and there was no way he could survive loving with every fiber and losing, as his father had. Women walked away from him as soon as they realized his profession was his first love. Eventually, Lizzie would too, and that wasn't what was best for her or Flora. He forced himself to lighten his grasp. "I have a demanding job. I've managed to make a name for myself, and traveling is the key to keeping my status."

"So you let status rule your days?"

"Like I said, I didn't set out with that in mind." She'd cut to the dirty truth: he'd settled for status over feelings. Over really living. "Things just fell into place." Or had he made sure to hold on to his wonder-boy status at all costs, because that was the only way he knew how to be?

"And now those things keep you away from your family, your father, and heaven help any woman who wanders into your life."

On defense, he fought to sound casual. "You bug the hell out of me, you know that?" He shared an annoyed though nonthreatening smile. "And you're far too accurate in your assumptions. Look, this is me. It's the way I live."

"Who says I want anything from you? In case you haven't noticed, I'm a new mother and I'm searching for a job and my plate is pretty full. Truth is, I don't have room for you."

She'd taken his hint and run with it, immediately relieving him of any guilt or responsibility. How did she have such a knack for reading people? Maybe getting tossed from one foster home to another growing up taught a young girl to read people and to never get her hopes up for anything permanent. Back came the guilt in a rush. Didn't Lizzie deserve more out of life?

No. He really needed to stay out of her life so she'd have a shot at a real relationship with someone who cherished her and Flora. That person wouldn't be him. Life didn't work that way for him.

"I'm not good enough for you, am I?"

He couldn't hide his shock since that thought had never entered his mind, and yet it was the first conclusion she'd jumped to. "Good enough? It has nothing to do with that."

She laughed. "Am I about to hear the 'it's not you, it's me' speech?"

He could see right through her tough and cynical mask, but wasn't it better to let her down now than later when it would really hurt? As he thought of Flora's future and how she deserved a father who loved her his heart sank. That baby had already managed to steal his heart, but that wasn't the point; they both deserved a better future than he could give them. He might be able to offer wealth and protection, but they deserved to be loved, a feeling he'd lost the day he broke his neck. When he'd risked it all for love, he'd nearly killed himself. "Thought I'd already given it."

Her wry laugh offered relief from the tense moment and begged for him to join in.

"So," he said. "After tonight—" he said, hurting in a place he'd long forgotten.

But he'd only gotten half of his thoughts out before she rolled on top and straddled him. "Who says tonight is over?"

She ducked her head and nailed him with an open-mouthed kiss, and there was no argument from him. She'd made a great point about their night together. He'd been honest with her and she still wanted to make love. He wasn't about to talk her out of right now. His hand cupped the back of her head and he kissed her as if there were no tomorrow.

This kind of escape he could handle, as long as feelings didn't enter in.

But wasn't it already too late?

* * *

They'd barely woken in time to shower and make their flight home, Sunday. An uneasy tension wove between them on the airplane, nearly erasing the amazing night they'd spent in each other's arms.

Lizzie watched out the window as they flew over Wyoming, her heart swelling at the beauty. Such wide-open spaces. A little piece of heaven she wanted for her and her daughter. As they landed she thought about her odds at getting placed in one of the programs from the administrators she'd met the night before.

Cole had set her up for more possibilities than she could ever dream up herself, yet she couldn't quite get Monty's comments from their last horseback ride out of her mind. What kind of future did she want for Flora? Her little fantasy about Cole would never play out. It had been foolish of her to even dream it up, because it already hurt like hell and there was nothing she could do to move Cole out of his lifelong rut. Now all she wanted was to get home to hold her baby again.

She glanced at Cole, diligently reading a cardiac-medicine journal, wishing things could be different between them but knowing better. She was a big girl, after all. Besides, his noticeable indifference this morning proved he hadn't been lying last night. There wasn't room for her, and especially for Flora, in his life. The man was honest on all levels, even the tough-as-nails topics. At least she could always count on him for that.

Maybe she could still make an impact on one aspect of his life, though. Because she cared, she opened a topic he'd pushed aside years ago. "So you'll only be in Cattleman Bluff a couple more weeks. Are you planning to set things straight with your father?"

Cole lifted his head slowly, removing his stare from the journal and placing it on her. "Has he talked to you?"

"I didn't need it spelled out. All I had to do was observe."

"Hmm." He started to go back to reading and she wasn't about to let him get off with a single-syllable response.

"And Monty and I talk all the time—" his head lifted, though he didn't look at her "—but not about the trouble between you two. Nope. Like I said, I figured that out myself." She waited a moment to make sure Cole was still listening. "He isn't getting any younger, you know."

Cole inhaled, immediately seeming uncomfortable about the conversation. "And he'll settle for nothing less than having both of his sons completely change their lives in order to accommodate his dream. *His* dream. Do you understand how unreasonable that is?"

She glanced down at the hands in her lap, not wanting to step on anything Cole needed to say, but thinking at least he had a family. Didn't he understand how precious that was?

"Trevor never got out of town. He could have had a far more lucrative and respected career but he stayed in Wyoming after medical school and took his residency in family practice. He got strapped with the clinic in Cattleman Bluff, and has never left since."

"But he was with your mother the last days of her life, and he wouldn't have met Julie again if things had worked out your way."

He went immediately thoughtful on the first part of her response, quickly passed over it to her second thought. "True, but who knows what opportunities he's missed because of sticking around?"

"Is life only about opportunities or missed opportunities to you?" He went silent, so she prodded more. "What's wrong with family medicine?"

"Nothing, if that's what a person wants. But I always

got the feeling Trevor wanted more. And having my brother around still hasn't made Dad happy."

"I think it's because neither of you have taken an interest in the ranching business. Your father really has made a name for himself. I think he's worried all will be lost when he dies."

"Jack is perfectly fine at handling the everyday issues, but Dad really does need to find a partner to handle the business end of it. Raising prime beef doesn't mean squat unless you have places to sell it."

"Circle M steer may not keep their reputation if an outsider steps in."

"What are you getting at?"

"Don't you have any interest in your family business? It's given you all the *opportunities* you've had in your life, to use your favorite word. Isn't it time to give a little back? Like you said, your brother has stuck around and is keeping a promise to the community with the clinic. You seem very business savvy in the medical field because of TAVR. You've marketed it all across the nation. Like you said, you're always on the road."

"And that makes me a meat magnate, how?"

"Same skills. Connections. Just different product."

He tossed his gaze upward with an unbelieving expression. Maybe she'd knocked him sideways and he was ready to pull the oxygen down and take a breath or two, or maybe it was just good old impatience. She understood she had a way of drawing that out of people.

The plane finally taxied to a stop and they jumped up to grab their carry-on bags, putting an abrupt end to the uncomfortable conversation. All she could hope was to plant a seed in Cole's thoughts about his future. To somehow make a difference in his life, even if she wouldn't be in it. Because wasn't that what you did when you cared about someone?

* * *

Cole hoped neither Gretchen nor Dad would pick up on the change in his and Lizzie's dynamics when they arrived home and came through the kitchen. Though it would take nothing short of award-winning acting to avoid it. After greeting Monty and Gretchen, Lizzie rushed to gather Flora from Gretchen's arms and, after kissing the baby hello, took off for privacy to nurse her. He was surprised by his own surge of happiness at seeing that bright and sweet baby face, wished he'd had a chance to kiss her, too. Instead, he got down a glass and filled it with water, then drank. Tiberius hung back in the kitchen along with Gretchen, waiting for a report, no doubt.

"She did great," he said after he'd emptied the glass. "Those hospital administrators were eating from her hand. It'll only be a matter of time before the offers come in."

For some odd reason, both his father and Gretchen looked disappointed. Didn't they want the best for her as he did? He gave them a couple of seconds to say something, anything, but neither did.

"Well, I'm exhausted, so I'll see you at dinner." Cole had a long to-do list. He needed to make arrangements for several upcoming trips, one in particular including an in-service for doctors at the University of California at San Francisco. He'd be demonstrating TAVR, then assisting with the head of cardiac care; next he'd talk him through another procedure and finally be an observer, but ready to step in with any glitches. Once he certified that doctor, if the hospital brought this life- and cost-saving procedure into their facility, it would be a huge West Coast win for his premier cardiac procedure. The medical-device company he worked for part-time would send a substantial bonus check. Maybe he'd skip family dinner tonight.

Though as he headed for his room he couldn't keep Lizzie's intruding conversation on the plane out of his mind. As with hers, his time on the ranch was coming to an end, and he really should hash things out with his father once and for all. There was so much more to discuss than who was taking over the ranch so the man could retire, but he really didn't have the energy to tackle that today, thanks in no small part to her. God, he ached for her already.

He halfheartedly cursed Lizzie for bringing up the tough topic, while loving that she'd cared enough, knowing he couldn't very well sidestep that conversation much longer.

CHAPTER TEN

It ONLY TOOK until Wednesday for the first residency offer to come through for Lizzie. She whooped and hung up the clinic office phone, then raced to Cole's door.

"Linda Poles just called to say she has an opening for me!" There was no way she could keep the excitement out of her voice.

"Great!" Cole's response didn't sound convincing. "And since she's a woman, you can't claim I pimped you out." His sardonic smile made no attempt to involve his eyes.

"This is true." She wasn't going to let him drag down her moment of victory. Besides, this was a typical good news/bad news deal. "There's only one drawback."

Now she had his full attention. He rose from his chair, circled around the desk and stood a couple of feet before her, waiting for her to fill him in.

"I need to start next week."

The perplexed and downright sad look on his face, a complete contrast to moments before, nearly made her stomach zip-line to her toes, until he quickly covered it up. Saying it out loud drove the point home, though. She'd be leaving. Very soon.

"I…uh…um…" she stammered, trying to work out how to best phrase her words. "I tried to talk her into letting me finish my time here, but she reminded me the program began July the first and that I've already missed weeks. She said I need to get back to Boston and jump right in. I've got a lot of catching up to do."

"And, of course, you're thrilled to get back on old turf and start the program." He'd schooled his expression, and gave nothing away from his reaction. His true thoughts and feelings would never see the light of day around Lizzie. Showing enthusiasm as only Cole could, he flashed that charming smile.

She needed to let him know how she felt, though, which was near panic. "I'm scared witless. I've got to find a place to live, make child-care arrangements. Let my patients here know."

"Lotte can take care of that part." Picking up on how frantic she was, Cole dropped the facade and stepped closer, drew her near, took her into his arms and closed the office door. "You know I'll help any way I can."

"Thank you." She stood there in his arms, savoring the feel of him, touched all the way to her marrow by how she'd missed him since Saturday night. How could she just walk away from everything she'd only just found here? As he'd opened the door for her dreams, even if they were last month's dreams, he'd soundly closed it to anything between them. She had to remember that.

Since coming to Cattleman Bluff and meeting Cole, her goals had subtly shifted, but she couldn't very well say thanks but no thanks to Boston. *I'd like to stick around in Wyoming now, if you don't mind.* She couldn't refuse, after all of his work on her behalf. This was her one big chance to prove herself in a resident program. To eventually find a solid job in a good hospital. To make the best home she could for Flora.

"The MGH program probably has suggestions for housing," he said, "and I'll pay you for the full six weeks you were hired for."

"I can't let you do that."

His grip grew tighter. "You don't have a choice in the matter. I'm in charge of who I pay."

And that, unfortunately, summed up the position she was in with Cole, once again. She'd moved to Wyoming without a choice and now she'd leave the same way.

"Your next patient is in the room." Lotte tapped on the door, figuring out where Lizzie was.

"I'll be right there," she said, wanting to kiss Cole, but sensing he couldn't handle that any more than she could. "Thanks again," she said, stepping out of his arms, willing herself to be ready for the rest of the afternoon appointments. Because she had to be.

Cole bit back every natural reaction he'd had to the news of Lizzie leaving, and rendered an award-winning performance, if he did say so himself. And wasn't he getting damn good at that? As the afternoon went on, with spot conversations here and there while passing in the hallway, or entering or exiting patient rooms, he'd informed her he could pull some strings to find an affordable apartment in a decent part of town. Later, he'd told a bold lie and said he could even find the best child-care facility available for little Flora. He'd set up something with Dr. Poles and the residency program. Lizzie didn't need to know.

Keep telling yourself it's what's best for Lizzie. And Flora. The thought of not seeing those two bright and shiny faces every day pinched in his gut. Even now he longed to take Lizzie in his arms and show her how much he felt for her. He'd let himself grow too accustomed to both of them. And exhibiting the biggest failure of wisdom in his life, he'd spent the most amazing night making love to Lizzie. How right they'd been for each other. He could definitely grow accustomed to that.

She'd forced him to feel again; he owed her more than

he could ever repay. And since he'd already been monumentally unethical, he'd pay for Flora's child care and lie that it was free to the residents. He'd call Linda as soon as he finished his next appointment to set things up.

Oh, and there was one more call he'd make before he left work today. Larry Rivers. He had some questions to ask.

A bitter taste settled in the back of his mouth.

"I got Elisabete placed," Cole said, leaning back in his swivel chair, facing away from the door, feet propped on the desk corner. "She's in *this* year, not *next.*"

Larry praised him, but the accolades only made his stomach churn.

"One thing's been bugging me," Cole said. "Why have you been so invested in Lizzie?"

Silence. "My son fathered Flora. Elisabete could have had him arrested for what he did to her."

Cole closed his eyes and pinched the bridge of his nose. "I see. So this was nothing more than repaying a debt."

He listened briefly while Larry summed up his troubled son, then quickly changed the topic back to Cole working wonders, though Cole's gut churned over Lizzie's ongoing hard-luck story. All the more reason to rejoice in having helped her move on. So why did he feel so bad?

"Yes, yes. I know, Larry." He worked hard to hide his true feelings. "They don't call me the Wonder Boy for nothing. Is there anything I can't do? Sure. Listen, Larry, next time I'm in Boston you can buy me dinner." Cole glanced up in time to see Lizzie standing in his doorway, having obviously not already left work as he'd assumed, and hearing his every word. The hurt and betrayal covering her face nearly knocked him out of his chair. She took off.

"Listen, I've got to go." Cole hung up the phone, but

Lizzie had already made it to the door. He chased her out of the building, not knowing what in the hell to say, but having to say something. She'd practically made it to her car when he caught up.

The hurt he'd glimpsed inside had turned to anger. "Dr. Rivers was behind this?"

"He wants to help you just like I do." He didn't dare step too close.

"You sounded like you'd worked a miracle or something."

He studied his boots, speechless, deciding to be honest, because Lizzie deserved it. "He's been invested in what's best for you. I needed something to take my mind off your leaving. He offered me dinner, that's all."

That stopped her briefly, but the indignation quickly returned. "I hope you choke on that dinner." She swung the car door open and got inside.

He stepped out of the way when she started the engine and backed out of her parking space. There was no stopping her, and he had nothing left to say. He'd just blown every bit of trust he'd earned from her.

There was no hiding the tension between Cole and Lizzie back at the ranch that night. She insisted on eating in her room, and he copped out to feeling relieved he wouldn't have to face her again. Dad and Gretchen looked at him over dinner as if he were the grim reaper. He hardly touched his meal.

"If you'll excuse me, I've got some matters to take care of in my room." He pushed out his chair, preparing to get up.

"What's going on?" Monty didn't hesitate to ask.

Might as well come clean, though he'd been waiting for her to break the news. "Lizzie got a resident spot in Boston. She'll be leaving this weekend, I suppose."

"And you're going to let that girl walk away?"

In what way did his father mean? Evidently he hadn't done a very good job of hiding his feelings for her. "It's out of my control," he said as he tossed his napkin on the table, trying his best to act nonchalant. He left the dining room, but not before he heard his father's final words on the matter.

"Like hell it is."

He hadn't been able to talk to Dr. Poles during clinic hours, but had arranged to call her that night. After bargaining with the Massachusetts General Hospital doctor over how best to provide for Lizzie without her knowing, he put his full attention to making arrangements for his upcoming trip to San Francisco. Anything to keep the sorry circumstances and the pain out of his mind. He booked a first-class flight and made reservations at a five-star hotel. It was after eleven when he heard Flora crying. He stopped briefly from updating his mobile-phone calendar to listen. The baby didn't stop crying, and it was reminiscent of when she'd first arrived.

Had colic come back with a vengeance? Was Flora picking up on Lizzie's tension?

He stood in his room listening, waiting, wondering what to do.

After five minutes the wails escalated. The poor baby sounded in pain. Gretchen had gone home for the night. Someone needed to help Lizzie. He opened his bedroom door and shot down the hall, and found Lizzie in the living room pacing the floor. Flora was safely secured, arms and legs dangling from the snuggly baby carrier wrapped around Lizzie.

Stress diffused from every inch of Lizzie's body. Her brows pressed down, near panic shown from her eyes.

"She's got a fever, but I don't know what's wrong with her. She never got fevers with colic."

"Did you look in her ears?"

"They seemed okay."

"You want me to double-check?"

"She's starting to calm down. I don't want to upset her again."

"What's her temperature?"

"One hundred and two."

"Did you give her acetaminophen?"

"A half-hour ago. It hasn't made any difference yet."

He wanted to go over to her, put his arms around both of them, to magically make things better, or at least help calm things down, but knew he'd only upset Lizzie more if he got close. So he stayed where he'd planted himself, and worried. "Anything going around at her child care?" He kept his voice level, unimposing.

"Gina didn't say anything."

"No cold or rashes?"

She just shook her head, exhausted and pushed to her limit.

"Let me take Flora for a while. Your back is probably tired."

Lizzie looked torn, but her weariness won out. "Okay." He undid the fastener of the baby backpack and slid it from her shoulders once she knew he had hold of everything. "Let me help you," she said as she adjusted the straps to meet his bigger size, and he cupped little Flora's bottom even though she was safely snug inside.

Without thinking, he bent and kissed her head, the fine black hair tickling his nose. He'd missed holding her, smelling her, wanting nothing more than to protect her from whatever it was that hurt. "It's okay, sweetheart. We'll figure something out here."

Once Lizzie knew everything was under control, she

sat in Monty's chair, hanging her head in her hands. "I'm no good at this. She gets sick and I quit thinking like a doctor, go right into panicked, helpless-parent mode."

Having never had a fatherly bone in his body, he'd learned a few things over the past few weeks. He knew babies liked to be walked around and lightly bounced or rocked. He also understood how precious a small child was, which nearly blew his mind, but mostly scared the daylights out of him. "It's hard to be clinical when your heart is invested so much. Family members change things, so don't be hard on yourself."

"How am I going to handle being a single mother in that program?"

Why was she doubting herself now? She'd always given the impression of pushing full speed ahead at all costs. That she could handle anything in her way. Why was she suddenly questioning herself? Maybe because she'd grown since coming here, just as he had. Maybe he'd helped her see the importance of making the right choices. What she needed right now wasn't a philosophical discussion on the matter. She needed support. "Same as you've handled it here. With backup. I've heard they've got child care for the hospital employees, even a sick bay for the little ones."

"I won't be able to af—"

"It's offered for residents. The single mothers anyway." So he lied just a little—hadn't he already blown her trust? In Lizzie's case, it *was* being offered. She didn't need to know he was paying for it.

"Do you think she could have a bladder infection?"

She'd started grasping at straws, but if it was her way of coping he didn't want to get in the way. "That's a possibility."

"Can we take her to the clinic and do a urine test?"

He stopped walking and rocking. "We'd have to catheterize her to get the specimen. You just said you get crazy when it's your flesh and blood, and I sure as hell haven't catheterized a baby since medical school. Are you sure you want to put her through that?"

Her face dropped with the prospect of having to wait until the morning with a sick baby, to find out what might be going on. Worry converged with fear and Cole suspected Lizzie might be on the verge of tears.

He snapped his fingers. "Hey, let me call Lotte. She's a whiz at pediatric procedures."

"It's eleven-thirty. We can't ask her to come in."

"Sure we can. We just can't demand she come in." He took out his cell phone and dialed her number. "Knowing her, she'll do it, though."

Twenty minutes later, Cole turned off the alarm system at the clinic and let them all in. Lotte hadn't hesitated an instant to offer to meet Lizzie and Cole to test Flora's urine. He'd had a hunch it would work that way. As Lizzie removed Flora from the baby carrier, Lotte gathered her supplies and Cole stepped out of the room rather than watch. No way.

Within two minutes, and with minimal crying from the wee one, Lotte handed him a jar of urine out the door. "Go test that," she said.

He dutifully took the specimen to the clinic minilab and dipped the test strip in it. Sure enough it was positive for nitrites, a byproduct of bacteria. "It's positive," he called out, then smiled when he heard Lizzie consult Lotte for what liquid-suspension antibiotics they had on hand. Practical as always, the nurse recommended a cephalosporin, right down to the amount per kilogram of Flora's weight and the number of ccs needed per dose.

Lizzie gave Flora the first dose before they left, and as Cole and she were packed up and ready to leave, Lotte sent them off with one more tidbit.

"Now, don't freak out when her poop looks maroon. It's just a side effect of the drug."

They both laughed with relief.

"Thank you," Lizzie said, her confidence in mothering secured once again since her hunch had been right. She glanced at Cole and smiled for the first time since that afternoon before overhearing his phone call. "I know you said I needed to tap into the older nurses as great sources of practical information. Now I'm a believer. My God, she was a genius at catheterizing my baby. No way could I have done that."

Not wanting to push their delicate circumstances, Cole simply nodded. He knew in his gut, as far as the two of them were concerned, he'd already stomped on any trust she'd developed in him, and that was something he couldn't change. For now he'd settle for relief that little Flora was going to be all right as soon as the medicine kicked in.

Saturday had come sooner than Lizzie could imagine. She sat on the corner of her bed, nearly all packed, trying to ward off her emotions, praying she could keep control until she left. But she couldn't help but go over the past twenty-four hours' events. Yesterday, she'd been overwhelmed by the number of former patients who'd stopped in at the clinic to send their regards and give thanks. Even Valerie's mother had made a special point to thank her for diagnosing and treating her daughter's migraines with a sock-it-to-me cake. To the best of Lizzie's understanding, everything but the kitchen sink was part of the recipe.

She'd come back to the ranch with her arms full of cooked and baked items, deciding to share them with the ranch hands rather than let them go to waste. Everyone's kindness had nearly brought tears to her eyes at the clinic, but she'd fended them off…until it had been time to say goodbye to Lotte and Rita and the rest of the help at the clinic. The rush of tears had surprised her as she'd hugged each person goodbye. It hadn't taken long at all to get attached to them, almost as if she belonged there.

Lotte had grabbed her and held tight. "You've got what it takes, Dr. Silva. We could use more doctors like you around here."

Coming from the crusty older nurse, it had meant the world and gave her confidence she could handle the residency in Boston, too.

When she'd picked up Flora from daycare, a second stream of tears had sprung, forcing her to realize how much she trusted and liked Gina, who'd started out as a patient and had quickly become a friend.

She'd miss Cattleman Bluff more than she could imagine.

Lizzie smoothed her hand over the comforter on the bed. She couldn't allow herself to think about Cole. This interim assignment was over, she'd gotten more out of it than she could ever have hoped for or dreamed of and now it was time to leave. Heck, packing and leaving had been her specialty growing up. Plus she'd always been good at hiding her emotions when it came time to leave. She could do this. Hell, she had to!

Now, of course, it took longer with packing for two, plus adding all the times she'd had to stop to dry her eyes. Thankfully Gretchen took Flora for her while she finished.

She came to the gorgeous blue dress in her closet and her thoughts shifted. She'd thought Cole was a man with great potential, but had changed her mind now. Sure, he was a brilliant doctor, but he fell far short of the mark as a son, and pity any poor unsuspecting woman who dared to fall for him. Like her. His disconnect with his feelings was beyond repair and there was nothing she or anyone else could do to fix it. Nope. She'd learned that lesson early on with her mother's drug addictions. That task would have to be his and his alone.

Forgetting about herself for a moment, she switched her thoughts to Tiberius and Cole, and she said a little prayer they'd work something out soon, before it was too late.

She glanced at her watch. Five more minutes and the packing was done. She dreaded having to face Tiberius and Gretchen for the last time, not to mention Cole. Oh, God, she couldn't go there. Not just yet. The dull ache she'd been carting around all morning in her chest suddenly pushed up a notch. She used her palm to massage the area between her breasts. Prickles started behind her lids. Again. Leaving a place where she'd grown to feel completely welcomed would be the hardest thing she'd ever had to do. After saying goodbye to Cole.

Leaving the man she'd accidentally fallen in love with would take every ounce of courage she possessed. Did she have enough? To save face she'd do everything in her power not to let on about her truest feelings. No matter how hard or seemingly impossible. She patted her cheeks and took a deep breath. *Keep it together, you have to.* Then rolled her baggage into the living room.

Cole was quick to relieve her of that duty. "I'll put these in the car," he said, not making eye contact, and for that she was grateful.

Gretchen had already started crying, even while holding Flora on her hip. "This place is going to feel so empty without the two of you, Elisabete." She reached for Lizzie's head and pulled her down to her level, then kissed her cheek. "I'll miss you. Please come back to see us."

Lizzie had to be honest. "I'll see how that goes. I can't promise anything right now." Tears streamed down her cheeks and she wiped them away with both hands. "I'll miss you, too. But I'll keep in touch online and I promise to send pictures and videos of Flora, okay?"

Gretchen hugged Flora close, snuggling her neck and kissing her chubby cheek. "I'm going to miss you so much, sweet potato. Don't forget your old granny Gretchen."

The two women circled Flora for a group hug and cried until they both felt embarrassed, then laughed uneasily and wiped at their wet faces. What else could they do? She had to leave.

"Are you about done?" Tiberius waited impatiently for his turn. "Come over and say goodbye to me, girlie-girl. We haven't got all day."

Lizzie turned and wandered into Monty's surprisingly open arms, unable to turn off the faucet. He hugged her as if he was a bit out of practice. When his mouth was close to her ear he said in a low voice, "Don't forget our little talk."

"I won't. I promise. How can I thank you for everything?"

"By being happy. Make that little one a happy home, okay?"

She hugged him like a sloppy drunk, *I love you, man*, not caring what he thought. "Yes, sir."

Tiberius's eyes watered when she pulled back her head, and she read every bit of sincerity in his wish for her just by looking into his craggy old face. So this was how it felt to be loved. Wow.

"I hate to break things up—" Cole's cautious voice cut through their moment "—but you've got a plane to catch."

She couldn't deny the truth. Maybe they'd have some time to talk things through on the drive to the airport, because it would be completely awkward otherwise. She hoped they would anyway.

He took Flora from Gretchen's hip and led the way out the front door…to a limousine?

"I've already put her car seat in place in the back."

Was the man serious? He wasn't even going to drive her to the airport?

Lizzie wanted to kick her own butt for being so stupid and hopeful. She'd actually thought she'd gotten through to him on some level, but his calling a car service to drive her off his property, the same way she'd arrived, proved that the only thing inside his chest was a cement block.

Well, two could play this ridiculous game. Egged on by anger, she shored up every last nerve and willed herself not to react. "Okay. Thanks." She refused to look at him as she got into the back of the town car. Only after she sat did she glance his way.

To his credit, he did look sad...*ish*. The one last thing she'd have to do was chuck every single good feeling she'd let sneak through her usual barriers for Cole and keep this goodbye strictly business.

"Thank you for giving me a job when I needed it the most." *Even if it was only because you had to.* "I'll never forget it." *Or you.* "Or Wyoming."

"You're welcome." His voice gritty, his hand grazed her fingers as he closed the car door, then, rather than move it away, as she expected, he covered her hand briefly with his, his warmth quickly spreading up her arm and fanning out across her shoulders. "I know I've been an ass, but I *will* miss you."

"Ready to go, sir?" The driver was behind the wheel checking his watch.

"Yes, yes."

"Okay, then." She didn't have a clue what to say next. *I forgive you? I love you?*

"Oh, there'll be another chauffeur in Boston. He'll have a sign with your name at the baggage-claim area. He'll take you to your resident quarters." He stepped back to let the limo pull out.

"Okay. Thank you for everything." *I'll never forget you!*

"Just be you and knock that hospital on its ear."

She couldn't help but smile at the implications of that comment. "And take care of your father," she called out the window as the car drove off, but not before she glimpsed a look of devastation on his face. He did care.

Cole stood watching the limousine drive off with the woman who'd changed his world as the corners of his life turned in on themselves, making him feel empty and dead. If he'd been hit by a car it wouldn't have hurt more than he did right now. But he had to let her go. It was for the best. For Flora's future.

Lizzie deserved better than him. He wouldn't stand in the way of that. Maybe, with this coveted residency in internal medicine, she'd finally put her life on track and become the huge success she'd worked diligently for all these years.

Maybe, with time, the crater in his chest would heal without her.

Tiberius and Gretchen instinctively knew better than to go near him just then. They'd waved goodbye to Lizzie from the porch as she'd driven off. Now they'd disappeared inside.

Cole stepped slowly into the ranch house, then found himself walking toward Lizzie and Flora's room. He could still feel her here, but knew this too would fade with time. He curled in his lips and pressed hard, damned if he was going to let himself react to the roiling deep in his chest. He hated that she could make him remember how impossibly hard it was to lose someone you...loved.

He inhaled, hoping for one last whiff of her before she vanished forever, then glanced toward the opened closet. Empty except for one item.

She'd left behind the blue evening gown. So she wouldn't have to remember their one night together?

Or to make sure he'd never forget?

CHAPTER ELEVEN

Two weeks later. San Francisco.

COLE MADE A SMALL incision near the premedicated hand-picked patient's groin to gain access to the femoral artery. The surgical nurse handed him the special sterile catheter. Cole took the stainless-steel stent with its attached trileaflet equine pericardial valve with fabric cuff and threaded it through the vein, using fluoroscopy to follow the venous path on the X-ray screen. It was a long and tedious process traveling from the groin to the heart, and it required meticulous technique and total concentration.

Several minutes later, once he reached the diseased valve in the patient's heart, Cole advanced the sheath from the femoral artery, steering around the aortic arch and through the stenotic valve. He made it look easy, but this was his specialty and he'd trained for years, perfecting the technique long before becoming a TAVI evangelist.

As instructed, the surgical team used rapid cardiac pacing to reduce cardiac output while he introduced and inflated the balloon that delivered the special prosthetic valve. He carefully positioned the new prosthetic valve adjacent to the calcified natural aortic valve and secured it in place. Then waited for the new valve to take over.

Angiography and echocardiography were performed

to assess the patency of the coronary artery and the new valve competency. All checked out as per his plan, and he began to remove the catheter. Once completely out of the patient, he surgically repaired the access site in the groin. When he was done, the surgical RN placed a pressure dressing over the incision and a five-pound sandbag over that to prevent bleeding or hematoma formation.

As the team finished the procedure, Cole discussed the success with the head cardiologist.

He'd just saved a man from open-heart surgery and the hospital thousands and thousands of dollars with a minimally invasive procedure that required a short recovery and little time in the hospital. It was a win-win situation and the way of the future and, most important, he believed in it.

He stepped out of the surgical suite and changed clothes. Later he'd meet with the team to discuss the procedure and to offer time-saving techniques, as well as a critique on their performance.

He'd spend the next few days here teaching the procedure to the few qualified cardiology staff members. Once he was positive they could perform the percutaneous aortic valve implantation on their own, he would certify them and his job would be done.

The first doctor on the list was a female cardiologist who reminded him of Lizzie. He'd thought of her every single day since she'd left the ranch. He'd started to call her several different times, but left well enough alone. She probably hated him, and, after the way he'd detached himself from their relationship, he couldn't blame her. She'd never understand it was for the best. Her best. Which reminded him: he'd gotten a disturbing message from his bank, saying that his automatic payment to Massachusetts General Hospital for Flora's child care had been returned. He needed to find out why.

First he called his bank to clarify the message, then he called Linda Poles at MGH for an explanation.

"She left," was Linda's exasperated response.

"What? What happened?"

"She changed her focus and took a residency at another hospital."

"Where?"

"Wyoming. Cheyenne."

Cole needed to sit down. He'd bent over backwards to accommodate her and she'd turned her back on the prestigious placement for...

He scratched his head; the only resident program he knew about at Wyoming University Hospital was for family practice, not internal medicine. His brother, Trevor, did his residency there. They were always searching for more residents.

What in the hell was going on? With trepidation, he called Lizzie, amazed by how moved he was just hearing her voice on the mobile answering system. He'd missed that fun accent. Her. God, he'd missed her, cursed himself every single day for letting her go. But he'd kept telling himself it was for the best. For her and Flora's future.

Maybe if he kept repeating it, he'd eventually believe it.

"Hi, Lizzie, this is Cole. Just got some surprising news and wanted to verify it with you. Call me when you can."

A few days later, it was almost time to board the plane back to Baltimore. Lizzie had never returned his call and it was driving him crazy. Was this her thumbing her nose at him or had she strategically put herself in Cheyenne to be closer to him? Laramie was only forty-two miles away. He'd spent enough time kicking himself for doing the wrong thing, and now, as illogical as it seemed, he needed to set some things straight. To finally do the right thing.

He stepped up to the gate counter to make an inquiry with the booking clerk.

* * *

Lizzie promised this move would be the last. Thank heavens she didn't own any worldly goods beyond all of Flora's things. Wyoming University Hospital agreed to let her rent a furnished room in the dorms for the married students. The apartment was tiny with one bedroom and a galley kitchen, but by her standards it was perfect, and she could walk to work every day. Also, the university had a child-development center that accepted Flora into their care program at a steep discount. If these weren't all signs she'd made the right decision, she didn't know what other proof she needed. She was back in Wyoming, and this would be home to her and Flora for the next three years, and after that? Well, she couldn't even predict day-to-day events, so that would be anyone's guess.

She hadn't returned Cole's call, couldn't, because she'd almost gone weak in the knees just hearing his voice. Obviously he'd found out about her abrupt change in plans. Well, it was her decision and she'd do what she felt best for her and her daughter.

She'd taken Tiberius's words to heart about his state needing more doctors. She'd had a long conversation with Trevor Montgomery over the phone about the pros and cons of switching from internal medicine to family practice, and he'd given a great endorsement for this program.

The oddest thing had happened when she'd flown back to Boston after spending her summer in Cattleman Bluff: she'd felt completely out of place. She'd been born and raised there, yet a little over a month in Wyoming had opened her eyes to a different kind of life. A life with big skies and clean air, miles and miles of wide-open land, ranches and horseback riding, where life slowed down and the people were down-to-earth. She felt cramped back home, but here a girl could stretch out and breathe. She liked it here.

Check that. She loved it here. She hummed content-edly while putting away the last of Flora's clothes as her baby napped.

There was a tap at the door, and, eager not to disturb Flora, she rushed over to open it. Her stomach dropped to her knees when she saw Cole on the other side. He'd cut his hair recently and looked tan. He wore a brown Western-style suit with an expensive-looking white polo shirt. From the tips of his boots to the top of his head, he looked all man, and his brown, cutting eyes nearly sliced through her. Yeah, he was angry.

"Don't get mad," were her first words, even knowing it was way too late for that. "I listened to my heart and this is where I needed to be."

He shook his head and stepped through her door. She got the message he wasn't the least bit glad to see her, but if that was the case, why did he come here?

She'd totally messed up his efforts at finding her a resi-dency, she'd essentially spit in his eye, rather than show gratitude, yet not for one second did she fear that he might manhandle her. He wasn't anything like her ex.

"Does this have something to do with my father?"

"If you had any kind of relationship with your father, you wouldn't need me to answer that."

He cocked his head, narrowing one eye. "Are you say-ing he did have something to do with your decision?"

"Contrary to your assuming you can call all the shots, I make all my own decisions. Your father just pointed me in a different direction."

"Are you aware Laramie is only forty-two miles away?"

"I thought you spent most of your time in Baltimore, and, besides, your living one town over shouldn't be a problem since you're always traveling. No worries about running into each other." She raised her hand in an oath. "I promise to stay out of your way."

He stepped closer and she couldn't budge. Nor could she breathe. All she could concentrate on was the face she'd missed so deeply; she had dreams about it every night.

"Forgive me for being cold to you," he said. "I never expected to—" He stopped.

"To what? Try to control my life? Use me to prove your Wonder Boy status?" Yes, she was still angry.

Not listening to her jeers, he studied and reached for her hair, lifted and dropped it back onto her shoulder, as if reacquainting himself with it. That simple act sent an avalanche of chills down her body. She prayed he wouldn't notice.

"To fall in love with you," he said, low and grainy, as if coming to this conclusion had worn him to the bone. "I never expected to love you."

She let the magic words settle in the air. She breathed them inward, savoring the feel of them, trying them on for size, deciding they fit perfectly with her feelings for him. But he didn't deserve to get off that easily. He'd thrown her life into chaos, then let her go without lifting a finger.

He'd broken her heart! "You wanted to get rid of me— you forced me to leave. Didn't even have the decency to drive me to the airport. How can I believe you?"

With nothing less than an agonized gaze, he dropped to one knee, reaching into his pocket and pulling out a ring. "This was my mother's engagement ring, and her mother's before that. I'd like you to wear it, to be my wife. Will you marry me?"

Wait, wait, wait. None of this made sense. He loved her and wanted to marry her? She must be hallucinating. "You kicked me out of your bed and sent me out of state. Why the change?"

There was that agonized expression again. "I'd gotten too used to being around you. I still needed to hear your voice…see your face…hear Flora coo." He started to stand up, but she pushed on his shoulder to keep him on that knee. So distracted by his confession, he didn't notice and stayed where she'd put him. "I want you with me. I have to be with you."

She wanted to stay angry at him, wanted him to hurt as much as she had when he'd let her leave. But he'd just as much as told her he'd been miserable without her, had missed her enough to come after her, knowing how angry she was, and ask her to marry him. He loved her.

Realizing she wasn't jumping right in with a yes, he added more. "I just cancelled my flight from California to Baltimore, to fly to Cheyenne, then drove out to the ranch to get this ring to ask you to marry me. What more proof do you need? Can you at least give me an answer?"

Okay, she wasn't imagining this. Cole was reverting back to his usual demanding self. But not before he'd begged her forgiveness and admitted how he felt. Thank God!

Seeing the big man on his knee, risking his pride by asking her to marry him completely out of the blue, and knowing without a doubt he meant it, undid her. She dropped to her wobbling knees before him and cupped the hand that offered the beautiful, delicate antique ring. "You can't keep messing with my life, Cole Montgomery."

"I promise to stop if you say yes."

She laughed through her tears. "Like hell you will."

His slow smile broadened, forming those natural brackets on either side of his cheeks. She loved that grin.

"Yes, I'll marry you." He freed his hand from hers, reaching for her shoulders so he could tug her closer and share a kiss that felt as if he'd been saving up since the day she'd left Cattleman Bluff.

She wrapped her arms around his neck and gave him a

kiss he'd never forget either because that was what a girl did when she loved a man with all her heart.

Moments later, she tore away from his mouth. "But first you've got to promise to have that talk with your father."

"Now who's messing with whose life?"

"You needed a kick in the ass on behalf of Monty."

"Before I hold you to marrying me, maybe you should know that I'm giving up the TAVR teaching. Already talked to Trevor about joining his practice. I won't have nearly the prestige I do now."

"Wow. You really have changed! That's the best news *evah*!"

"So you love me, then?"

"You know I do."

She dove for him and knocked him backwards, then picked up the kiss where they'd just left off. After wrestling to get her hand, Cole slid the ring onto her finger, and it fit surprisingly well, as if it had been made for Lizzie. "I love you," he said, again.

"I love you, too." Thrilled to the core, she stopped and admired the platinum, gold and diamond ring with those dewy eyes. He looked on with pride, love surging through his veins, just as Flora woke up from her nap with a shriek.

Cole's brows shot up. "Mind if I get her up?"

"Be my guest." She rolled off him.

"You think she'll remember me?" He squeezed her arm affectionately as he got up.

"It's only been three weeks," she said as he helped her stand.

He walked lightly into the bedroom, Lizzie following behind, and he spoke softly. "Hey, little Flora bear, it's Cole."

The baby squealed with delight when she saw him, and relief circled his body. "Hey, she's sitting up—when did that happen?"

"Last week. Look a little closer."

He did, and with the baby smiling he saw her first tooth. "Look at that—you're growing up!"

Lizzie came up beside him, stretching her arm around his back. "Since we'll be getting married, maybe from now on you should call yourself Daddy?"

Cole lifted Flora, kissed her chubby cheek, then turned his megawatt smile toward Lizzie. "I like the sound of that."

The next night Cole sat down with his father in the living room at the ranch. Lizzie had blackmailed him into doing it by refusing to sleep with him until he did. But as she said, there was no time like the present, and he really couldn't argue with that advice. This conversation was way overdue.

"Can I get you some tea or something?" Cole said, hoping to steal more time to gather his thoughts.

Tiberius scrunched up his face. "You got something you want to talk about or not?"

So that was how it was going to be, but, honestly, did Cole actually think things might be different? He sat and leveled his gaze on his father, trying not to notice the butterflies in his belly. "As a matter of fact, I've got a lot of things to talk about. First off, I've asked Lizzie to marry me and you're the first to know."

The shocked double take almost made Cole laugh. "Well, that's the first display of good sense I've seen from you in years." His old man smiled and shook Cole's hand, after delivering the backhanded compliment. "Congratulations."

"Thanks. I'm glad you approve. And I think you already know you played a role in it."

"I didn't want that filly to get away. She's a real catch. And you're way past your time to get married."

Rather than take offense, Cole focused on what really mattered most. "She reminds you of Mom, doesn't she?"

Tiberius nodded thoughtfully. "She'll be good for you."

"Agreed." They sat in silence, enjoying the rare truce.

His father cleared his throat. "You know, neither of us ever wanted to admit it, but we're a lot alike."

Cole shook his head. "Don't I know that. Mom had her hands full trying to keep peace in the house."

"That's 'cause you were always trying to prove how tough you were."

"And you never did that, right?"

Tiberius nodded mildly, a small smile creasing his lips spawning an expression packed with memories. "I'd come off the rodeo circuit and survived, assumed you would, too. Didn't your momma call you Wonder Boy?"

"Maybe it went to my head a little." The toughest memory of his life flashed before him. "I sure as hell never expected to break my neck."

"Yeah, you went and let that horse almost throw you into a funeral parlor, and—"

Cole knee-jerked the challenge; he leaned forward to make his point. "I didn't let it happen, it just happened." Yeah, his voice might have sounded gruffer than he'd meant.

"You made a poor choice that day, riding bareback for that *girl*."

"I was fifteen." *I had just made love for the first time in my life the night before with the girl of my dreams.* Yet he couldn't deny the truth. "And you never did anything stupid when you were young, right?"

"Like I said, we're a lot alike. That's why I've always been so hard on you. That's why I expected you'd take over the ranch one day. I couldn't believe how you dumped anything to do with horses, rodeo and ranching after you broke your neck."

Cole wanted to scrub his face in frustration, but he sat still, willing himself to stay calm and talk this out with his father, not to let this conversation turn into a yelling fest like all the others. "I found a different calling, Dad." He changed the tone of his voice. "I honestly believe I was meant to be a doctor."

"And you had to drag your brother along, too."

"That was his choice."

Cole could see the fight slip out of his father. "And now I'm getting too old to run this ranch and I don't have anyone to step in, to keep it running, just a couple of fancy doctors for sons."

Cole couldn't let the slight slide by. "You know, I do save lives. How come I've never gotten the feeling that you respect what I do?"

"Of course I respect what you do. I'm proud of you, always have been, but that doesn't fix my ranching problem, does it?"

Cole rested his elbows on his thighs, waiting to make eye contact with his dad. Wasn't this the perfect example for how he'd learned to be selfish? "Not everyone is meant to be a rancher, Dad, not even the sons of the best rancher in these parts."

"You'd think that at least one of you would have taken an interest." Tiberius leaned his head against the cushiony chair, squeezing his eyes closed like a little frustrated kid.

"You've got the best man for the job right under your nose and you can't even see it."

"Trevor?" One eye popped open. "Hell, he's too busy with the clinic and my grandson and that new wife of his."

"Jack, Dad. Your foreman knows this ranch inside out. He's been working here for, what, twenty years?"

Now both eyes were open and ready for a fight. "Of course he knows the ranch but he doesn't have an ounce of business savvy."

"Trevor's good with bookkeeping."

"I'm talking about connections. Finding new venues to sell our steer for meat. Without buyers, we're nothing. We won't have a future. Do you know how many people are vegetarians these days?"

Cole chuckled. It had never occurred to him exactly how many hats his father had worn running Circle M all these years. It wasn't just about tending steer and selling them for the best price—he had set up the buyers and accounted for all the business investments along the way, too. Not to mention raising his boys and taking care of his wife. Hell, the man had probably only taken three vacations in his entire adult life. His health was waning and he couldn't keep up anymore. Cole weaved his fingers together and thought that was the sad and undeniable truth. He finally understood it was time to pitch in and help, just as Trevor already had.

"I've got connections all over the country. You tell me what you need, and I'll do my best to open some doors for our steer. We can make this a family business, but with the help of Jack. Isn't it about time you made him a Circle M partner?"

He could see the surprise and glimmer of hope in his father's milky eyes at the prospect of making Circle M Ranch a group business. A small corporation. Maybe it wouldn't be a traditional family business, as he'd always hoped for, but wasn't that the way of the world now?

"I'll think about it." Tiberius crinkled his brow, already considering the change.

Cole reached across and squeezed his father's forearm. "Dad, one more thing." How should he put this? Probably best to keep it simple, and straight. "I haven't told you nearly enough. Hell, probably never." He waited for his father's gaze to rise so he could look him in the eyes. "I admire you. You made something out of your life. You started out with nothing. Not many people can claim that. In case you're still wondering, I do respect you."

He'd hit home on that one. His father's eyes got watery, his lower lip quivery as the compliment sank in. "And I've always been proud of you, Cole. Sorry I wasn't so good at showing it."

"Like I said, or was it you who said it?" A wry smile twisted Cole's lips. "We're a lot more alike than we'd ever like to admit."

In the next second Cole felt a cool hand on top of his, and something about his father's bony grip warmed a huge and growing area smack in the middle of his chest.

EPILOGUE

Two months later. A cool and crisp Saturday afternoon in autumn...

FOR THE SECOND TIME in four months Cole wore a suit and waited for a wedding to start. But this was a brand-new Western-styled tuxedo, not that other city-style deal with the bad memories. The small group of guests gathered near the mossy pond beside the cluster of Glory Red maple trees on the Circle M Ranch.

Tiberius had promised a big surprise and instructed Cole to quit looking at his watch and enjoy the day. He stood beneath the portable seven-foot pergola draped with sparkly white chiffon and bright-colored Gerbera daisies, breathing in the chilled air and letting it calm him. Was he really getting married one month before his forty-first birthday, to a woman only halfway through her twenties?

He grinned to himself. You bet he was, and she was the most beautiful woman in the world, as a matter of fact. The best choice he could ever make.

He glanced at his soon-to-be daughter, dressed like a little white fairy in the arms of his new sister-in-law, Julie, then noticed the tiny silver slippers Flora wore and grinned even more. He'd never totally understood the word *cute* until he'd met that baby.

Trevor waited at the back of the rows of chairs instead of standing by his side as his best man. Cole figured there must be a reason and stood where he'd been placed like a good unquestioning boy. A first!

Tiberius had agreed to walk Lizzie down the aisle—if you could call a path covered in windblown autumn leaves an aisle. The guests sat on white vinyl foldable chairs that Trevor's son, James, had spent all morning setting up. The rows were crooked, seeming more diagonal than straight, but what did Cole expect from a thirteen-year-old? And they served their purpose. He wasn't about to complain.

Soft Celtic string music started playing through speakers and all eyes traveled toward the grove of trees on the opposite side of the pond. Cole's pulse jumped as he watched and waited for his bride.

Slowly emerging from the ash and maples came one, then two young women dressed in cocktail-length dresses, red like the leaves on the maple trees. Lizzie had chosen her two newest friends to be her bridesmaids. Both had started out as acquaintances at the clinic but one had become Flora's caregiver, Gina, and the other was Rita the receptionist. This time around, instead of catching the bouquet, Rita got to carry one.

Next Zebulon walked between the trees and, just as Cole wondered what in the world the horse was doing there, the most beautiful sight Cole had ever seen appeared. Lizzie sat sidesaddle, straight and confident, her flowing white dress blanketing the horse's entire back, loins-to-tail and all the way down his belly. The ball-gown cut of her dress made a wide V across her shoulders and dipped to the top of her breasts. A thick, sparkly pearl belt cinched in her waist. She didn't wear a veil, just a feathery flower on the side of her head, and Cole was happy to see she'd left her hair down, with tiny braids weaving an intricate pattern around her head. Breathtaking. Especially knowing that beneath that dress she wore the garter he'd caught at his brother's wedding. His heart had never felt as full as now, with this vision of his soon-to-be wife.

So that was what all those Saturday-afternoon horseback rides with his father were about. Lizzie had embraced Wyoming life with a vengeance since they'd gotten engaged and she'd committed to becoming a family-practice doctor like his brother. The old ranch hadn't felt this much like home since his mother had died. He glanced upward—*I hope you're watching*—then to the front row.

In honor of Lizzie's grandmother and her favorite foster mother, Janie Tuttle, two chairs had been left empty on the bride's side. A third reserved chair had been placed on the groom's side for his mom.

With Zebulon pacing the bridesmaids, and the violin music swelling, Lizzie held the reins comfortably and single-handedly, wearing elbow-length fingerless white lace gloves. With the other hand, she held a fire-burst-colored bouquet.

She circled the mossy pond under the bright blue sky, with occasional puffy white clouds floating overhead, trees in a range of fall colors surrounding her and the hauntingly romantic music drifting on the wind. A perfect moment. The love of his life was coming to him, to take her vows to love and honor, as he would her. He'd cherish her no matter what lay ahead, never more determined to put another person's needs and desires before his own.

It occurred to Cole that his father and brother both understood, and he'd never felt closer to them than right now.

His brother met Lizzie at the back of the chairs as the bridesmaids paced the makeshift outdoor aisle toward the arbor, where Cole waited. He couldn't take his eyes off her, afraid if he looked away this moment might disappear. Trevor lifted Lizzie from the horse, then let Gretchen adjust the train of the dress before she made her final walk down the aisle on the arm of her new father-in-law, the obviously proud Tiberius Montgomery…to him.

Lizzie's amazing green stare connected with his and melded, sending waves of love to ripple over him, her angelic smile stealing his breath. His father handed her over to him and stepped back as the pastor began the ceremony, but Cole couldn't quit looking at her.

Holding her cool, mildly trembling hand, he thought how fragile his bride was beneath her confident exterior. He promised to protect and treasure her, and as the rest of the vows became a blur he saw only Lizzie, until the pastor prompted him to say the best and most important words of his life.

"I do."

* * * * *

MILLS & BOON®
Hardback – October 2015

ROMANCE

Claimed for Makarov's Baby	Sharon Kendrick
An Heir Fit for a King	Abby Green
The Wedding Night Debt	Cathy Williams
Seducing His Enemy's Daughter	Annie West
Reunited for the Billionaire's Legacy	Jennifer Hayward
Hidden in the Sheikh's Harem	Michelle Conder
Resisting the Sicilian Playboy	Amanda Cinelli
The Return of Antonides	Anne McAllister
Soldier, Hero...Husband?	Cara Colter
Falling for Mr December	Kate Hardy
The Baby Who Saved Christmas	Alison Roberts
A Proposal Worth Millions	Sophie Pembroke
The Baby of Their Dreams	Carol Marinelli
Falling for Her Reluctant Sheikh	Amalie Berlin
Hot-Shot Doc, Secret Dad	Lynne Marshall
Father for Her Newborn Baby	Lynne Marshall
His Little Christmas Miracle	Emily Forbes
Safe in the Surgeon's Arms	Molly Evans
Pursued	Tracy Wolff
A Royal Temptation	Charlene Sands

MILLS & BOON®
Large Print – October 2015

ROMANCE

The Bride Fonseca Needs	Abby Green
Sheikh's Forbidden Conquest	Chantelle Shaw
Protecting the Desert Heir	Caitlin Crews
Seduced into the Greek's World	Dani Collins
Tempted by Her Billionaire Boss	Jennifer Hayward
Married for the Prince's Convenience	Maya Blake
The Sicilian's Surprise Wife	Tara Pammi
His Unexpected Baby Bombshell	Soraya Lane
Falling for the Bridesmaid	Sophie Pembroke
A Millionaire for Cinderella	Barbara Wallace
From Paradise...to Pregnant!	Kandy Shepherd

HISTORICAL

A Mistress for Major Bartlett	Annie Burrows
The Chaperon's Seduction	Sarah Mallory
Rake Most Likely to Rebel	Bronwyn Scott
Whispers at Court	Blythe Gifford
Summer of the Viking	Michelle Styles

MEDICAL

Just One Night?	Carol Marinelli
Meant-To-Be Family	Marion Lennox
The Soldier She Could Never Forget	Tina Beckett
The Doctor's Redemption	Susan Carlisle
Wanted: Parents for a Baby!	Laura Iding
His Perfect Bride?	Louisa Heaton

MILLS & BOON®
Hardback – November 2015

ROMANCE

A Christmas Vow of Seduction	Maisey Yates
Brazilian's Nine Months' Notice	Susan Stephens
The Sheikh's Christmas Conquest	Sharon Kendrick
Shackled to the Sheikh	Trish Morey
Unwrapping the Castelli Secret	Caitlin Crews
A Marriage Fit for a Sinner	Maya Blake
Larenzo's Christmas Baby	Kate Hewitt
Bought for Her Innocence	Tara Pammi
His Lost-and-Found Bride	Scarlet Wilson
Housekeeper Under the Mistletoe	Cara Colter
Gift-Wrapped in Her Wedding Dress	Kandy Shepherd
The Prince's Christmas Vow	Jennifer Faye
A Touch of Christmas Magic	Scarlet Wilson
Her Christmas Baby Bump	Robin Gianna
Winter Wedding in Vegas	Janice Lynn
One Night Before Christmas	Susan Carlisle
A December to Remember	Sue MacKay
A Father This Christmas?	Louisa Heaton
A Christmas Baby Surprise	Catherine Mann
Courting the Cowboy Boss	Janice Maynard

MILLS & BOON®
Large Print – November 2015

ROMANCE

The Ruthless Greek's Return	Sharon Kendrick
Bound by the Billionaire's Baby	Cathy Williams
Married for Amari's Heir	Maisey Yates
A Taste of Sin	Maggie Cox
Sicilian's Shock Proposal	Carol Marinelli
Vows Made in Secret	Louise Fuller
The Sheikh's Wedding Contract	Andie Brock
A Bride for the Italian Boss	Susan Meier
The Millionaire's True Worth	Rebecca Winters
The Earl's Convenient Wife	Marion Lennox
Vettori's Damsel in Distress	Liz Fielding

HISTORICAL

A Rose for Major Flint	Louise Allen
The Duke's Daring Debutante	Ann Lethbridge
Lord Laughraine's Summer Promise	Elizabeth Beacon
Warrior of Ice	Michelle Willingham
A Wager for the Widow	Elisabeth Hobbes

MEDICAL

Always the Midwife	Alison Roberts
Midwife's Baby Bump	Susanne Hampton
A Kiss to Melt Her Heart	Emily Forbes
Tempted by Her Italian Surgeon	Louisa George
Daring to Date Her Ex	Annie Claydon
The One Man to Heal Her	Meredith Webber

5 GEN STD LP

MILLS & BOON®

Why shop at millsandboon.co.uk?

Each year, thousands of romance readers find their perfect read at millsandboon.co.uk. That's because we're passionate about bringing you the very best romantic fiction. Here are some of the advantages of shopping at www.millsandboon.co.uk:

* **Get new books first**—you'll be able to buy your favourite books one month before they hit the shops

* **Get exclusive discounts**—you'll also be able to buy our specially created monthly collections, with up to 50% off the RRP

* **Find your favourite authors**—latest news, interviews and new releases for all your favourite authors and series on our website, plus ideas for what to try next

* **Join in**—once you've bought your favourite books, don't forget to register with us to rate, review and join in the discussions

Visit **www.millsandboon.co.uk**
for all this and more today!